SHADOW QUEEN

Treadwell Supernatural Directive Book Two

ORLANDO A. SANCHEZ

BITTEN PEACHES
PUBLISHING

© 2023 Orlando A. Sanchez

Published by: Bitten Peaches Publishing

Cover Art: Deranged Doctor Design www.derangeddoctordesign.com

Website: www.orlandoasanchez.com

ABOUT THE STORY

Beauty is only skin deep, but evil goes down to the core.

In order to fulfill his blood debt to Heka and the Word-weavers, Sebastian needs the Sacred Amethyst—an artifact of immense magical power capable of shifting a mage to Archmage.

To get it, he must acquire the gem from Maledicta, a darkmage group of assassins led by Calum Kers, a pyromancer who will destroy anyone who stands in his way.

Starting with the Treadwell Supernatural Directive.

There's only one complication.

Calum and Maledicta no longer possess the amethyst, the Shadow Queen does.

Sebastian believes the Shadow Queen is really Regina Clark.

Regina Clark is beautiful, intelligent, ruthless, and deadly. An ex-member of the Treadwell Supernatural Directive, she and Sebastian share decades of history...good and bad.

Mostly bad.

As a world-class thief and darkmage, she seeks power—

the power of the Sacred Amethyst. She will do everything in her power to obtain the Amethyst, even if it means betraying Sebastian and letting him fall to Calum and Maledicta.

Now, Sebastian must face Regina, retake the amethyst, and stop Maledicta before the Directive is destroyed, and Regina escapes with millions and a priceless artifact.

"Love is merely a madness, and, I tell you, deserves as well a dark house and a whip as madmen do."
-William Shakespeare

ONE

I floored the accelerator as Tiger opened the window.

We raced down the FDR Drive in the middle of the night as several vehicles gave chase. They were running out of patience and we were running out of road.

The Tank was designed to take damage, hence the name. It wasn't designed to outrace everything. That being said, Cecil had planned for contingencies. The only issue was we didn't have the several miles of open road I needed to activate those contingencies on the FDR.

The two vehicles behind us were closing in as Tiger reached into one of the weapon compartments and pulled out an Eradicator. It was one of the weapons Goat had designed for the Directive. If an RPG could be reduced to hand cannon size and fire the equivalent of bazooka shells, that would be an Eradicator. It was designed for breaching operations.

Tiger wanted to blow up our pursuers and chunks of the FDR.

"I told you this was a bad idea," she said as she opened fire and missed, the recoil nearly throwing her out of the Tank. "These idiots don't know when to quit."

"Have you ever used an Eradicator before?" I asked, grabbing her by the waist with one hand, and pulling her back into the Tank as I swerved around the light traffic. "Do you even know how to use one?"

"What's to know?" she snapped back. "Point and destroy. How hard can it be?"

"Put that thing away before you destroy the entirety of the FDR," I said. "I'm not going to explain to Ursula how you managed to rip up several miles of roadway. You know the DAMNED are not exactly the patient types."

Machine gun fire ripped across the side of the Tank. I swerved to the side to avoid the next barrage of bullets.

"Shit," Tiger said, ducking beneath the open window as rounds punched along the passenger side of the Tank. "That was close."

"They're using conventional weapons?" I asked, accelerating down the FDR. "Really?"

"I didn't say they were smart, just determined."

"It seems they don't like you. Any reason why?"

"Don't ask *me* why they hate me, ask *them*."

"I would, but they seem to be speaking your language —violence."

More machine gun fire raced across the rear of the Tank.

"If they even scratch the finish," she said, "I'm going to introduce them to pain. I just had her detailed yesterday."

"This is what happens when you end a conversation by burying your claws in someone's stomach."

"He drew a blade on me," she explained. "What was I supposed to do? Let him think he could get away with that? Not in my reality."

"How far away is Ox?"

"Three minutes," she said. "He's coming up behind them."

"We'll run out of the FDR in three minutes," I said. "Can you slow them down?"

"Stop the Tank," she said, her voice determined. "I'll slow them down."

"Tiger..." I said, shaking my head. "I didn't ask if you could slaughter them. Can you slow them down without a wholesale massacre?"

"You doubt my skill?"

"At wholesale slaughter? Not in the least. At restraint? I wonder if you even know the meaning of the word."

"I know restraint," she said, her voice dark. "Stop the Tank and let me show you."

"I am so going to regret this," I said under my breath as I brought the Tank to a stop and turned it sideways, blocking two lanes on the FDR. "Leave the Eradicator."

She placed it in the weapons compartment.

"I wasn't planning on using it," she said, stepping out of the Tank and into the roadway. "You coming?"

"Minimal damage to the FDR would be good," I said, stepping out of the Tank. "As it is, I'm going to have to make a call to the DAMNED."

"Minimal damage to the FDR and maximum damage to these idiots," she said with a smile that promised pain. "Works for me."

"Do *not* kill them," I said, standing next to her. "They may have information we can use."

"Unlikely."

"Tiger...Alive."

"Fine. Broken, bloody, and bruised, but alive."

I nodded and glanced behind us. The Brooklyn Bridge loomed in the background, illuminating the night as the FDR Drive split into several off- ramps in the distance, heading to Lower Manhattan.

Two black BMW M5s screamed down the FDR heading

straight at us.

"I wonder what the strategy is?" I asked as the cars bore down on us. "Maybe they want to crush you?"

"Wouldn't be the first time," she said as she gestured and stepped forward. "I doubt it will be the last."

The air shimmered in front of her as a wall of energy raced forward to intercept the cars. Tiger's inherent ability as a kinetic mage lacked any overt energy manifestation. Her casts didn't glow or produce light of any kind. It's what made her ability so dangerous.

It was difficult to counter what you couldn't see.

Both cars slammed into the kinetic wall of energy. They didn't come to an immediate stop, which would have jettisoned the drivers through the windshields, most likely ending their lives in the process. Rather, Tiger designed her wall to 'catch' the cars, slowing them down as they approached.

Even with her precaution, the front of both cars crumpled as they impacted her cast, appearing as if a giant fist had punched them. It wasn't too far off from the truth.

Tiger looked at the cars in disgust.

"German engineering at its finest," she spat. "What is that, carbon fiber? May as well make them out of tissue paper."

"Nice catch," I said as the cars slowed to a stop. "I'm impressed."

"See?" she said. "I know restraint."

"I stand corrected."

In the distance, I saw a large black van closing in on us.

Ox.

The passengers who were eagerly trying to fill us with bullets minutes ago, opted to remain in their vehicles with the doors locked. Tiger cast again, creating another wall behind the cars, preventing them from reversing, and effectively trapping them between the walls of energy.

"You want to do the honors?" Tiger asked. "Or should I?"

I peered into the cars and saw that each vehicle contained three passengers. Their energy signatures were negligible which meant they were low threat security.

"Not a mage among them," I said, walking to the cars. "What exactly did you say to them? I mean aside from skewering the one who drew a blade on you?"

Tiger approached the car on the left.

"I asked them if they had heard of a group called Maledicta," she said. "Then they got all stabby."

"I doubt these are part of the group," I said as I drew close to the left car. "Dark mage assassins don't use machine guns. They prefer to unleash deadly casts."

Tiger stepped close to the car and tapped on the window. It remained closed with the window up.

"Open the door, or I open it for you," she said sweetly. "Trust me when I tell you that it's better and safer if you open the door."

The driver's door opened a crack.

"Throw the weapons out," she said, this time not as sweet. "If you so much as point one of those machine guns in my direction, this car becomes your coffin, and I shove it into the river."

To make sure they knew she was serious, she raised a hand, whispered some words while slowly making a fist. The air around the car hardened and began crushing the car, making the streamlined design even more streamlined as it was crushed from the sides.

The men inside quickly opened the windows and tossed their weapons out. She turned to the second car which was several feet away and they, too, threw their guns onto the roadway.

"See? They may be misguided, but they aren't suicidal," she said. "Drivers, out."

When the driver hesitated, probably due to fear, she pointed at the driver's door and slashed her arm away, ripping the door from the car. The driver stumbled out with the force of the cast.

"That's a little over the top, wouldn't you say?"

"Nothing like fear to get a point across."

"Or make them completely uncooperative," I said. "Tone it down a bit. They aren't a threat."

The driver slid back on the ground, away from Tiger, with a look of fear on his face. He backed up into the car, his gaze remaining transfixed on the door which lay several yards away.

"How? How...how did you...did you do that?" the driver stammered. "That's not possible."

"Normals?" Tiger asked, peering down at the driver before shaking her head. She turned away and headed to the other car. "They're all yours."

I approached the driver.

"What's your name?" I asked as I drew closer. "Who do you work for?"

"Patrick. My name is Patrick," he said. "I can't tell you. He'll kill me if I tell you."

I felt a surge of energy coming from both cars simultaneously. Tiger, who was next to the other car, turned her head suddenly and shot me a glance.

"Get back!" she yelled as she hit me with a cast that propelled me away from the cars. "It's a—!"

I landed hard on the far side of the Tank and rolled for several feet. She never got to finish her sentence. I managed to get to my feet and saw her cast a shield as both BMW M5s exploded with her standing between them.

The shockwave from the explosion knocked me back farther. Tiger managed to walk over to me, stunned and bloody.

"When I said broken, bloody, and bruised—I meant them," she said, slurring her words. "Damn, that hurts. I'm going to need a moment."

She leaned on the Tank and sank to the ground.

She had managed to harden her skin and took the brunt of the blast with minimal damage. Her body had started healing, but she was still dazed and slightly out of it.

The explosion had taken both of us by surprise. I walked around the Tank and headed to the charred wrecks that used to be the BMWs.

All of the passengers were unrecognizable. The flames had burned them nearly to ash, which meant it was no ordinary explosive device. Nothing burned that hot, that fast, without affecting everything around it.

This flame targeted the humans.

Someone didn't want us to know who they were, and was willing to kill to keep their identity hidden.

Now *this* felt like Maledicta.

TWO

Ox pulled up several minutes later.

He stopped the van several feet away from the charred vehicles and stepped out. He wasn't wearing his usual suit since we had alerted him to the tail only a few minutes after we noticed them. Instead he was in a black T-shirt, jeans, and brown work boots—what Tiger liked to call his construction worker outfit.

It meant he had gotten dressed in a hurry.

He walked over to the vehicles and examined the bodies.

"Not even an Eradicator would do this kind of damage," Ox said, peering at the cars. "Boss?"

"I am not in the habit of barbecuing people to death," I said, mildly offended. "Besides they didn't pose that kind of threat."

"Just checking," he said. "You are wearing a dragon's mark. Char's mark, to be precise. Didn't know if that came with a flame thrower option."

"It doesn't, at least not to my knowledge," I said, pointing at the vehicles. "They were carrying explosive devices and were remotely detonated. See if you can salvage anything."

"I'll have my crew take the cars back to the Church," he said, pulling out his phone and peering at the bodies. "What do you want to do with them?"

"I'll call Haven," I said. "Roxanne can send over some of her people to deal with the remains. In the meantime, place the bodies on the side until EMTes get here."

"Poor bastards," Ox said, shaking his head. "Not a good way to go."

"At least it was fast," Tiger said. "They had maybe a second before it was over."

Ox nodded as he looked behind him at the damage to the FDR and whistled low.

"That is going to snarl the morning commute," he said, shaking his head. "Who's going to call the Bear?"

"I'll call Ursula," I said. "Get the hauler here and remove those cars. I want a full forensic report on whatever is left of those devices, how powerful and what cast they used. Have Goat look into it."

"Will do. Did you say cast?" he asked, looking at the cars again. "They used runic explosives?"

"My best guess is yes," I said. "Targeted all organic material in the vehicles, left the cars mostly intact."

"Runic bombs aren't cheap," he said, pressing a button on his phone. "Two, maybe three, suppliers in the city."

"Tiger and I will pay them a visit," I said. "If there's a connection to this Maledicta, it will be there."

"Doubt they would purchase it direct," Ox said, then looked down at his phone. "Not if they're trying to hide their tracks like this."

"True, but even with a middleman and several cutouts, the purchase of runic explosives is difficult to hide."

"We could always go ask Char," Tiger said. "I'm sure she would know, or at least knows someone who knows."

"I'd rather not disturb her with this," I said. "We'll go see her if we run into a dead end with the suppliers."

"You just don't want her to chastise you for not figuring it out yourself," she said. "I can hear her now: *Bas, you come to me with this? Even a child could figure this out. Remove yourself from the Dungeon.*"

"I doubt she would be that gracious," I said, thinking about Char's reaction. "Ox, how long until these cars are gone?"

"Hauler will be here in five minutes, he said. "You better get DAMNED down here ASAP. They might even have this fixed before rush hour."

"Unlikely," Tiger said, returning to the Tank. "By the way, could you pay *The Dirty Faucet* a visit? That's where we picked up this tail."

"Anything specific there?"

"Maledicta," she said. "I doubt these victims had a direct line to them, but they became hostile once I asked about the group."

Ox nodded.

"I'll look into it, and have Rat do some sniffing around," he said. "If we find out anything, I'll let you know."

"Thank you," Tiger said, getting into the Tank.

"She okay?" Ox said as I heard the sound of a large truck headed our way. "She seems a little tense."

"Regina is in town," I said. "Need I say more?"

"Regina?" Ox said. "Would it be possible to request some vacation time before those two decide to shred each other?"

"If I have to stay here, so do you," I said. "This applies to the entire Directive. Make sure they know I will not accept any sudden onset of mysterious illnesses."

"Got it, Boss," he said as the hauler came into view. "Better take care of this. I'll see you back at the Church."

"Once I find the supplier, I'll let you know," I said. "Be careful with those vehicles."

"Will do," he said and turned to face the approaching hauler. He motioned to the driver. "Over here."

I pulled out my phone and headed over to the Tank.

Morning was several hours away, and we had a runic explosives dealer to track down. This information would be difficult to obtain; most of the individuals who trafficked in these kinds of munitions weren't the sort to share information about their buyers.

The driver's side window slowly dropped and Tiger glared at me to hurry up.

"Where to?" she asked as I strapped into the passenger side. "The Casbah?"

"Yes, Altair is usually meticulous about who he sells to," I said. "I can't see him providing these bombs, however—"

"If it wasn't him, he would know who did," she said, starting the engine. "Casbah it is."

I nodded as she pulled away from the wreckage and headed downtown.

THREE

I dialed the first of two calls I needed to make.

"Sebastian," Roxanne said as the call connected through the Tank. "Who died?"

"What would make you say that?" I said. "I could simply be calling to—"

"You never simply *just* call," she said. "It's either someone is gravely injured or deceased. Which is it and where?"

I really needed to become less predictable.

"FDR Drive south, right before the Brooklyn Bridge," I said. "Six victims, all deceased."

"Is this your doing?" Roxanne asked, then paused. "No, this doesn't sound like you. Who upset Tiger? I presume she can hear me?"

"Yes, she can. No one upset her," I said, glancing at Tiger who wore a slight smile. She worried me sometimes. "We were investigating a lead. They were following. When we detained them to get information, they were remotely detonated."

"Remotely detonated?" she asked. "Do you know what kind of detonation?"

"Organically targeted runic explosive device," I said. "Flash fire killed them in less than a second, but left the vehicles mostly intact. Have you ever seen something like that?"

"Unfortunately, yes," she said, her voice tinged with anger and sadness. "We called them flashcasts. Not very common these days. I've never seen it with an explosive device, however. That would require an experienced pyromancer with a significant expertise in explosive devices."

"Hello, Roxanne," Tiger said as she avoided traffic. "Any reason these flashcasts aren't used as a delayed explosive more often?"

"They're too dangerous. Flashcasts require advanced pyromantic knowledge," Roxanne answered. "Placing a cast that unstable in an explosive device is a good way to get cremated. They are highly volatile."

"Got it," Tiger said. "Would you know the range on one of these casts?"

"A flashcast, like many advanced casts, requires line of sight to be effective," Roxanne said. "It's very difficult to incinerate a target without seeing it."

"We're on our way to see Altair now," I said. "He may have some information."

"Altair?" Roxanne asked, her voice dark. "You're going to the Casbah?"

"Yes, seems like the safest approach."

"It's not," she said. "I'll send you his home address; it would be safer if you approach him there. He has a tendency to surround himself with individuals that would view your visit to the Casbah as overt hostility. Besides, he wouldn't be at the club at this hour."

"I'm fine with overt hostility," Tiger said, her smile widening. "You have his home address? How do you know he isn't at the club?"

"I wasn't always the Director of Haven," Roxanne

answered, the tone in her voice ending that line of questioning. "I'll send it over now with the understanding that going to his home is only slightly less dangerous than visiting him at the Casbah."

"Any chance Altair is behind this device?"

"It's unlikely," Roxanne said. "He stands to lose too much if he's implicated in something like this. That being said, it's not impossible. If he didn't create it—"

"He would know who did," I finished.

"Yes. As far as I know, he wouldn't create something like this, but he is one of the most, if not the most experienced pyromancer in the city," she said. "He can't be trusted. Be careful."

"I will be," I said. "Ox is on site at the FDR, removing the wreckage. If you need assistance with the bodies, don't hesitate to reach out to him."

"EMTes are en route. My people will take care of it," she said. "I'm glad this wasn't you or Tiger. I'll send Tristan your regards."

"Please do, and tell him to stay away from Verity for the foreseeable future," I said. "They will be undergoing some restructuring in their management, and I don't want him getting any more of their attention."

"Sebastian, what are you planning?"

"Have to go," I said quickly. "Always a pleasure."

I ended the call.

"Nice of her to think of me like that," Tiger said as I dialed the second call. "It's nice to know my reputation precedes me."

"Maybe it wouldn't precede you if you reined in your casts a bit more," I said. "There's much to be said for subtlety."

"My casts are feral," she said. "They're in your face, giving you a bloody nose, maybe a black eye, with a lost tooth or two. They're not like your casts—self-important and pretty. I don't do pretty...ever."

"I think the word you're looking for is refined."

"No, the word I'm looking for is snobbish," she said as Altair's address appeared on the dash."Toffee-nosed, if that doesn't make sense to you."

"I am not snobbish in any way, shape or fashion," I protested. "Toffee-nosed? Really?"

"Speaking of fashion, why don't you just wear a T-shirt and a pair of jeans?" she asked, glancing at me. "Ox and Honor pull it off, especially Honor. He *really* pulls it off. You could learn a thing or two from his fashion sense."

"You better not let Rahbi hear you refer to Honor that way."

"They have a thing?"

"I don't know and I've never asked."

"Because it wouldn't be proper?"

"Exactly, it would be the height of impropriety—"

She just gave me a mischievous grin.

"Like I said, snotoffee-nosed."

"That's not even a word."

"It is now," she said. "Are we really going after Verity?"

"Yes," I said, looking out of the window for a few seconds. "They destroyed the White House and tried to eliminate us. Not responding to an overt act of violence against the Directive sets a dangerous precedent. I have Goat preparing a response for them."

"Goat?" she asked. "Can I deliver this response?"

"Absolutely not," I said. "They will know it came from us, but we can't be seen to be directly involved—at least not yet."

"That why you sent Tristan the warning?"

"That, and he has a tendency to fight fair."

"That's a good way to get yourself killed in our world," Tiger said. "No one fights fair and everyone is cheating."

"That's how we stay alive," I said with a nod. "He was raised a Montague, which means a much nicer worldview. Treadwells are raised slightly differently; leverage, information, and lethality prove more effective when walking in the darkness."

"Taking on Verity is not operating in the shadows, though," she said. "That's going to get noticed."

"I know, which is why he needs to stay away," I said. "When it starts, they will know, and they will retaliate. I prefer to have them direct their ire in our direction."

"Good, I liked the White House," she said. "I've been looking forward to having a conversation with them since the renovation."

"In due time," I said, raising a finger, as I made the second call.

"Decons And Magical Nulls-Elite Division. Ursula speaking."

FOUR

"Ursula," I said, connecting the call to the Tank. "Good evening."

"It was, until I answered this call," she said. "Where and how bad?"

"FDR Drive south near the Brooklyn Bridge," I said. "Ox is on site, but the damage is a little farther north from his location."

"That's near three nexus points," she said. "Extent of damage? What caused it? Runic or conventional?"

"Conventional," I said. "Several rounds from an Eradicator that missed their target." I glanced at Tiger who refused to look in my direction. "And destroyed the roadway instead."

"Eradicator?" Ursula asked, frustration in her voice. "Last time I checked, the FDR wasn't a hardened bunker that needed breaching. Has that changed?"

"It hasn't," I said. "Someone was a bit overzealous in an effort to stop a target."

"Right," Ursula said, letting out a long sigh, "so I'm going to assume this was your calm and stable second-in-command."

"Yes, you assume correctly."

"What made her think that firing the equivalent of bazooka shells into one of the most traversed parkways of the city, walking distance from a cluster of three nexus points, and several hours before rush hour was a good idea?"

"You have my deepest apologies."

"Did you fire the Eradicator?"

"No."

"Then your apology means nothing to me," she said. "Your apology isn't going to fix the FDR now, is it?"

"No, it's not."

"I know she can hear me," Ursula said. "I can hear her breathing."

Ursula was the Lead Director and Nexus Keeper of the DAMNED—the Decons And Magical Nulls, Elite Division. She was also a werebear who was immune to most magic and possessed heightened senses, making her a considerable threat.

That was without factoring in her weapon, a runed hammer she supposedly *borrowed* from a thunder god, which made her nearly unstoppable.

Getting on her bad side was unwise.

I glared at Tiger who sighed after a few seconds and caved.

"I apologize, Ursula," Tiger said reluctantly. "My aim was off and I didn't factor for the recoil of the Eradicator."

"That wasn't so hard now, was it?" Ursula said. "There's growth in owning your mistakes."

Tiger glared daggers at me.

"Yes, Mother," Tiger said. "Anything else while I'm reconsidering my life choices?"

"You owe me a sparring session," Ursula said after a pause. "A *real* one."

Tiger smiled.

"You sure about that?" Tiger asked. "I'd hate to have to hand you your ass...again."

"Hasn't happened yet," Ursula snapped with a small laugh. "You give me the sparring session, and I might forget to include your name in my report. Your call."

I raised an eyebrow at Tiger.

In my effort to keep the Directive low-key and off everyone's radar, I had several standing agreements with the authorities to omit our involvement in the less-than-reputable activities that occurred in the city.

In exchange, we agreed to limit our presence and footprint to negligible levels. Blowing craters into the FDR was not considered limiting our presence.

"Fine," Tiger answered. "You leave your hammer at home, though."

"I would hate to have an unfair advantage," Ursula said. "Agreed, no weapons. I'll even let you cast."

"You would hate to have an unfair advantage?" Tiger scoffed. "Says the runically immune werebear?"

"I can't help what I am," Ursula said. I could almost hear the smile. "It's hard work being this amazing."

"Sure, just a heads up—we may be dealing with an explosives expert," I said. "So you may have more damage in the immediate future."

"Wonderful, it's not like I'm busy or anything, keeping the Mourn away from nexus points," Ursula said. "I'll send a crew over to the FDR. You keep me posted if there is more damage."

"We shall," I said. "Thank you again."

"You can thank me by not breaking my city," she said. "Between you and your cousin, it's a miracle there's anything left intact. Why don't you both go on an extended holiday?"

"You know precisely why we can't."

"I do," she said. "I can dream, though. I'd appreciate it if you would stop blowing craters into my streets. Tiger, call me with a date."

"Will do."

Ursula ended the call.

"That went much better than expected," I said. "She seemed unusually calm about the whole thing."

"Only because she's going to pound me into the ground, repeatedly," Tiger said. "I hate sparring with her."

"You brought this on yourself," I said, looking at the address on the display. "One second—is that the correct address?"

"Yes," she said. "Noticed that, did you?"

"Bloody hell," I said under my breath. "Altair lives there? You're certain?"

"Unless Roxanne has the wrong information," Tiger said. "Odds of that happening?"

"Slim to zero," I said, realizing we were heading into a proverbial lion's den. "She doesn't make those kinds of errors. I can't believe she thought that going to his home was safer than the Casbah?"

"Either the Casbah has become staggeringly lethal since the last time we visited, or Altair has downgraded the clientele in his club to the ridiculously deadly category, if Roxanne is sending us to Phoenix Hall."

"We can't just walk into the Hall," I said. "That would be a death sentence."

"I'm open to suggestions," Tiger said. "I'm not in the mood for getting blasted to bits for an unauthorized approach."

"The best we can do is let Altair know we're coming," I said. "I'll call the concierge."

"You have the number to the concierge of Phoenix Hall?" she asked. "Really?"

"Yes, it has proven useful in the past," I said, dialing the number. "I don't know if it will help in this instance."

"Of course *you* would have that number," she said. "Why am I not surprised?"

"It's information and a resource both are important currencies in our world," I said as the call connected. "This is not a pass. This will just prevent immediate hostilities as we enter the building."

"Good evening, Mr. Treadwell," an accented voice answered. "How may I be of service?"

"Good evening, Leland," I answered. "I need to pay the Hall an unsanctioned visit."

"You do realize we have a strict policy regarding visitors," Leland said after a pause. "If I may inquire, who would you like to call upon this evening?"

"Altair."

"I see," Leland said, his voice neutral. "Please hold."

The line became silent.

After thirty seconds, I heard a small cough over the line.

"Your request has been granted, Mr. Treadwell," Leland said. "When should I anticipate your arrival?"

"Five minutes."

"Very well," Leland answered. "I shall notify your host."

"Thank you, Leland."

"Good evening, sir."

He ended the call.

"How bad is it?" Tiger asked. "What are we walking into?"

"Phoenix Hall is a fortress masquerading as an upscale building," I said, thinking back to my experiences of the location. "Getting in without authorization is a suicide mission. The interior is filled with traps and failsafes."

"And getting out?"

"Worse than getting in," I said. "The Hall has formidable

security personnel and a building-wide null field, which can be deployed in minutes."

"They can shut down the entire building?"

"Yes. I only know one person who managed to escape that place unscathed. There's still a standing bounty on her head."

"*Her* head?" Tiger asked. "Wait, tell me it isn't—"

"Regina," I said with a nod. "Hopefully, that won't complicate things."

"As long as they don't believe in death by association, we should be fine."

"It was before the formation of the Directive," I replied. "She managed to liberate a valuable artifact from a resident."

"Liberate?" Tiger scoffed. "You mean she stole it."

"That's what I just said," I answered. "Still, there may be some blowback. Regina has a talent for making enemies."

"She has a talent for making enemies and leaving others hanging out to dry." Tiger said, heading to the 14th Street exit on the FDR. "The woman is a walking red flag. How you ever got involved with her still makes me wonder."

"It complicated."

"It's insane is what it is," she said. "I have a feeling this visit is going to rate high in the suckage factor. Maybe we *should* visit him at the Casbah."

"If Roxanne suggested his home, I'd advise we take her suggestion," I said. "I'm not in the mood to fight my way out of that particular club."

"So we're going to opt for fighting our way out of this fortress Altair calls home?"

"I'd prefer not having to fight our way out of anywhere," I said. "Think we can manage that?"

"Are you insinuating *I'm* the reason people are always trying to kill us?"

"You're not?"

"I mean, I am, but you don't have to rub it in. I'm just not looking forward to visiting Altair in his home. It puts us at a disadvantage."

"Only if you're planning to attack him," I answered with a sigh. "Are you planning to attack him?"

"I never say never," she answered. "I'll be diplomatic. I just don't like walking into traps, and this building screams trap."

"Well, we don't have a choice," I said, looking at the address again. "If Altair isn't part of our attempted detonation, his reaction should be irritable, but manageable."

"And if he's part of the attempt at our death by explosion?" she asked."Can I be diplomatic then?"

"We'll use tact until it's time to use violence," I said. "Hopefully it won't come to that."

"How have you managed to survive this long on the streets?" she asked, shaking her head. "If he's part of this, there isn't going to be time for tact. We need to use diplomacy."

"Unlike some people, I don't immediately presume the worst in everyone I interact with," I said. "Besides, there's always time for tact. You'll find fewer people trying to shoot, stab, or detonate you when you use diplomacy."

"I find violence to be extremely diplomatic."

"You keep using that word; I don't think it means what you think it means."

"It means exactly what I need it to mean, especially when I draw my claws."

I shook my head as we approached Gramercy Park.

FIVE

According to Roxanne's information, Altair lived at 36 Gramercy Park East, otherwise known as Phoenix Hall.

Located between E 20th Street and E 21st Street, with 3rd Avenue to the east and Gramercy Park East to the west, it formed part of the group of properties that surrounded the private park in the center of the enclave known as Gramercy Park.

The residents of these buildings belonged to various powerful factions operating in the city. Phoenix Hall housed the most dangerous and influential individuals to walk in the shadows.

It was rumored that even Char had a home in Phoenix Hall, though this had never been substantiated and no one had ever seen her near the property.

The Hall's location wasn't a secret, though its residents were. No one really knew who lived within its walls. The resident list was made up of rumor and supposition, which were unreliable at best.

The property possessed powerful runic defenses which deterred unwanted visitors. It wasn't surprising that Altair would live there. What did surprise me was that Roxanne had this information. I would need to have a deeper conversation about that with her at a later date.

Tiger pulled up to the front of the building and parked the Tank.

The building was designed in the French Gothic style, cladding the façade with inexpensive, white terra-cotta which easily molded into the detailed gothic arches, colonnettes, shields, cherubs, and gargoyles.

The building was the height of pretentiousness and reveled in it.

Standing guard in front of the entrance on raised stone pedestals were two full suits of runed armor, holding metal halberds with sharpened axe blades. It was my understanding that they acted as a line of defense when activated—a fact I had no intention of proving tonight.

"Those things real?" Tiger asked as she exited the Tank and glanced at the suits of armor. "They look dangerous."

"Because they probably are," I said, crossing the courtyard. "Those halberds are real, as are the runes etched into the armor. They're part of the defenses."

"Authentic suits of runed armor?" she said, pausing to admire the silent sentinels. "Well, excuse me, this is about as froufrou as it gets. Why don't we have a pair of these guarding the Church?"

"Because they are exorbitantly expensive—in material cost, runes, and upkeep. We have more practical defenses... like you."

"Oh, ha ha, humor," she said, shooting me a glare. "You think they can actually fight like a human?"

"Let's not find out," I said, approaching the main entrance. I paused at the door and allowed Tiger to catch up. "Do not antagonize Leland, and try to rein in the menace."

"Menace?" she said, feigning offense. "I'm the least menacing person I know."

"That doesn't help your case, considering the people you know," I answered. "When we meet Altair, let me do the talking."

She bowed with a flourish.

"Lead on, Sir Eloquence," she mocked. "I will be completely silent."

"Somehow I really doubt that," I said, placing my hand on the large wooden door. "Keep your eyes open, and treat this place as hostile until we exit the premises."

The door wasn't Australian Buloke. I gazed on it and realized that the exterior was wood, but the core was runed titanium, designed to withstand everything short of major ordnance.

"Door seems pretty solid," she said, looking at it. "Maybe I should bring the Eradicator."

"How about we start the evening by not antagonizing the very proficient pyromancer who lives here." I said, returning her glare. "We are not here to start a war. The Eradicator stays in the Tank."

"Fine," she said, raising her hands. "Just trying to be proactively diplomatic."

"Leave the diplomacy to me, thank you."

She nodded and focused on the runes on the door, which became a bright orange as I removed my hand. A few moments later, the door opened inward.

The interior of the lobby was mostly stone and marble. The rust-colored stones that made up the floor were covered with subtle defensive runes. A large wooden reception desk sat to the right of the lobby facing the entrance, with two large wingback chairs around a small circular table occupying the left side of the expansive space.

The lobby was brightly lit and showcased a large chandelier that hung over the reception desk. Leland, who stood behind the massive desk, wore a black, silver, and red accented uniform. Over the left side of his chest and on each shoulder, I saw the image of a flaming phoenix. He looked up when we stepped into the lobby.

With a nod of his head, he motioned to the elevator, which was opposite the reception area.

"Ninth floor, sir," he said in his deep voice. "I trust you will have a pleasant visit. Your host is waiting."

"Thank you, Leland," I said as we stepped into the waiting elevator. "Have a good evening."

He nodded again and went back to sorting some documents behind his desk. I knew the impression of mild aloofness he gave off was an illusion. Leland was a capable and highly skilled mage.

The elevator doors whispered closed as I pressed the ninth floor button.

"How well do you know Altair?" Tiger asked, examining the interior of the elevator. "I've only met him a few times at the Casbah. Never long enough to get a good impression of him."

"I know him well enough, I suppose—mostly by reputation," I said. "Shrewd in business, ruthless in battle. Not an adversary to take lightly. His enemies fear him and his allies respect him. He built up the Casbah from nothing into a hub of prominence within a decade. No small feat."

She nodded as we rose to the ninth floor, keeping her gaze on the ceiling of the elevator.

"Some nasty defenses up there," she said, still looking up. "This building takes its security seriously."

I followed her gaze with my own and saw the runic failsafes attached to the ceiling, cables, and sides of the elevator. From what I could make out, the elevator was designed to free fall as a result of a failsafe. It would make for a painful, if not deadly drop.

"It's designed to drop the passengers during a breach in the defenses," I said. "Can't imagine anyone would be foolish enough to ride an elevator during an attack."

"We're riding the elevator."

"True, but we are *not* currently attacking the building, are we?"

"Not yet, we aren't," she said. "It's still early and we haven't spoken with Altair. I'd say the situation is fluid."

"No, it is not fluid. We, I, will ask him some questions and then we will leave the Hall without changing the solidity of this situation. Understood?"

"I still think I should've brought the Eradicator," she answered. "It's a great deterrent."

"A weapon is only a deterrent if its capacity for destruction is respected by your adversary," I said. "Do you really think Altair would be deterred by a gun, even one as powerful as an Eradicator?"

"We'll never find out now, will we?"

At our destination, the elevator chimed and the doors sighed open. We stepped out into the hallway and saw only one door at the end.

"Only one door?" she asked as she looked around. "He has the whole floor to himself?"

"It certainly seems that way," I said, giving the hallway a cursory scan. "These older buildings have expansive floor plans. I'm sure he values his privacy, and paid for the privilege of maintaining it in his home."

"What else do you see?" she asked as we headed down the hallway. "How secure is it?"

I *looked* down the hallway, pulling down my glasses to use my innersight, and saw the defensive runes lining the walls, floor, and ceiling. Some of them were merely designed to stun and incapacitate; others, however, were lethal.

Altair took his security seriously.

"Substantially," I said. "Let's try and leave the way we arrived. Getting down this hallway alone will be a challenge if the defenses are active."

She nodded in response as we approached the door to Altair's home.

I knocked on the door and it silently swung open.

SIX

Altair's home was a sharp contrast to the overall pre-war gothic design of Phoenix Hall. Once we stepped inside, I took a moment to absorb the feel of the space.

We stood in a minimalist's dream home.

The walls were a mix of off-white and cream. Japanese kanji written on aged parchment hung on some of the walls in plain wooden frames. The floor, which was an aged parquet, gleamed in the dim lighting. There was a slight citrus smell in the air, which seemed to permeate the entirety of the space— present, but not overwhelming.

"I feel like Master Yat is going to pop out any moment in this place," Tiger said under her breath. "This place feels more like a dojo than a living space."

I nodded as we moved forward.

An empty corridor greeted us as the door closed behind us with a click. I felt the gentle surge of power as the door closed, completing a defensive barrier.

"Can you get through it?" I asked, keeping my voice low. "That barrier seems quite robust."

"Probably," Tiger said, her voice matching my tone as she

scanned the foyer. "You know what *could* get through it easily?"

"Don't."

"An Eradicator," she continued with a slight nod. "It's almost as if it was created for getting through barriers, just like the one that formed behind us. Imagine that."

"Your point has been made," I said. "I don't think we will—"

"Sebastian," a voice called out from somewhere ahead of us. "You and your second are most welcome. Please, come in."

"Sebastian?" Tiger repeated under her breath. "You're on a first name basis with him? You two friends?"

"No," I said. "We are, however, acquaintances."

"How did he know it was me?"

Tiger peered into the corners—looking for cameras, I presumed. We stepped into the large foyer without entering the space proper. This was an area to receive guests and was furnished with several small chaises to facilitate the removal and donning of footwear.

"He is an accomplished pyromancer," I said, admiring the foyer. "Your energy signature isn't exactly subtle, especially after what Char gave us."

"You have a point," she answered, still looking around. "Her mark doesn't assist in the concealment department."

"True, but the purpose of our visit here doesn't require stealth," I said, glancing down at the mark on my hand. "We will, however, need to address these marks. I'm sure Goat may have an idea."

"Do we even know what these things do?" she asked, "besides announce our presence?"

"Honor is compiling a list of possible capabilities," I said. "Apparently my knowledge on these kinds of marks is lacking, according to him. He will inform us when he is done with his research."

"So you don't know?"

"I have ideas, but marks like these vary considerably depending on who imparts them," I said. "I figured it would be good to get someone with experience and knowledge to explain what they can or can't do. I opted for a trusted source."

"The Librarian is your trusted source?" she asked. "And he agreed?"

"Yes. You know Honor," I said. "This is a mystery and puzzle for him. One he wants to unravel, with actual field tests."

"Great. He's such a geek sometimes," she said. "The last time we conducted a field test with Honor, people ended up in Haven."

"True. He does get a bit overzealous with his experiments."

"We could always just ask the dragon. She should know, don't you think?"

"I think if she wanted to share she would have," I said. "She takes pleasure in her riddles. I would hate to deprive her of her small joys."

Tiger looked at her hand.

"Her riddles have a way of being dangerous. She should've just told us."

"It may be her mark reacts to each individual in a unique manner," I answered. "She may not even know what the outcome will be until the particular mark manifests its properties."

Tiger gave me a hard stare.

"You really think she doesn't know or have an idea how her mark will interact with each of us?" Tiger asked. "She's old, not stupid. The very least she could've done is give us a heads up about it being detectable. I'm not a fan of my presence being announced...ever."

"I'm aware," I said. "You prefer to make your presence known with that signature trait that is so you...violence."

She smiled.

"Have you ever pondered that violence is a language everyone understands?" she asked. "I find that amazing. It crosses all language barriers instantly."

"A fist communicates more than a thousand words? That kind of thing?"

"Exactly," she said, glancing down at her hand. "Still, I'm not comfortable with this mark letting people know I'm coming."

"There's a good chance that he assumed that if I'm here, you wouldn't be too far behind," I said. "You are, after all, my second."

"I don't like being predictable," she said. "Predictability can get you killed."

"Agreed," I said, looking down at the small area where several pairs of shoes rested. I removed my shoes, placing them on the rug and pointing while giving Tiger a look. "Shoes."

"What?" she asked, looking at her shoes. "These are custom Louboutin Bifrosts. I had to make a special trip to Paris to purchase them. Christian personally oversaw the design."

"Thank you for that fascinating nugget of information. As riveting as that may be, I'm not asking you to discard them," I said. "Let's respect Altair's no shoes policy in *his* home."

"Oh, I will," she said, taking off the shoes, which looked more like weapons in her hands than high-end designer shoes, and placed them on the rug. "I was just letting you know who to see and where, should they need to be replaced."

"Duly noted," I said as we walked down the corridor. "I'm sure they're in no danger."

"For your sake, I hope you're right."

If Tiger had one weakness, it was her love of obscenely priced designer shoes. She had a particular preference for the red-bottomed soles created by Christian Louboutin.

When I inquired as to why she preferred these shoes almost exclusively to all others, she had replied that Christian treated her kindly. He listened to her requests, treating her like a person, not a client, or a threat.

It had made an impression on her and had garnered Louboutin her brand loyalty. I didn't question it, I just knew better than to come between her and her shoes.

We continued walking down the long corridor. It led into a smaller hallway on the left which opened into a large living room. On our right, was another small corridor which led to a sizable dining room.

On our way farther into the living room, before entering the living room proper, we crossed a set of sliding doors which were slightly ajar, revealing a spacious master bedroom.

The living room was sparsely furnished.

Covering the center of the polished parquet floor and dominating the space was the Pearl Carpet of Baroda. I paused for a moment to admire the artwork that was the carpet.

It was made up of gold, silver, silk, and natural pearls and complemented the rest of the room perfectly. I was under the impression that this carpet was supposed to be sitting in a museum somewhere.

This was either an incredible copy, or Altair had arranged for the original to be replaced by an authentic looking counterfeit, while the original sat in his living room.

Either scenario raised more questions than it answered.

A large fireplace on the left provided additional warmth to the inviting room. On the far side, opposite the fireplace, three large bay windows allowed views of Gramercy Park below.

The aesthetic of the home was a decidedly Asian fusion of Japanese and Indian influences. A large *horigotatsu*—a low Japanese table—dominated one corner of the space. The table sat on a large tatami mat surrounded by four *zabuton*—sitting cushions.

Around the room, several translucent shoji screens obscured the view of the windows and divided the space into small nooks. Along the walls of the living room were several sword holders, each of them holding *daisho*—katana and wakizashi, a set of long and short swords worn by samurai during the Edo period.

Above the fireplace was a single-sword display stand holding a sword in a blood red *saya,* or sheath. The sword in that particular stand held an exceptionally potent energy signature.

It was the kind of energy signature I didn't want to experience up close.

Tiger glanced at the sword over the fireplace and gave me a look I knew too well: *that thing is dangerous.*

I gave her a subtle nod in response. The sword over the fireplace was the infamous Crimson Flame, a blade supposedly forged in the heart of a volcano and merged with a fire shard.

I had never seen it wielded in battle, and according to the stories of its power, I never wanted to.

Altair, who was sitting at the table in the corner, was dressed in a comfortable indigo *yukata*—a light summer kimono with a decorative silver dragonfly motif.

It was difficult to gauge his age. He appeared to be in his early sixties. He kept his gray hair cut short and I could tell he kept himself physically fit from the way the kimono rested on his frame. His piercing dark eyes followed us as we entered the living room.

With a subtle gesture, he motioned for us to sit at the

table as he poured tea into *yunomi*—small, handle-less cylindrical tea cups.

"To what do I owe the pleasure of your presence this evening?" he asked. His soft voice crossed the room, carrying an edge of menace. He gave us a slight bow as we sat. "I rarely get visitors here, so I must assume it is an issue of some import that brings you unbidden to my home, when others would fear to incur my wrath."

The subtext was clear: *Why are you coming to my home uninvited and more importantly, why shouldn't I blast you to ashes where you sit?*

"Thank you for seeing us on such short notice," I said, returning the bow. I glanced over to see Tiger do the same. "We encountered—"

"Stop," he said sharply. "Your hands, extend them."

I extended both my hands.

"No. Each of you," he said, looking from Tiger to me. "Each of you extend your hand. The one bearing the mark."

Tiger and I extended our hands as instructed.

SEVEN

He narrowed his eyes at us.

He took our hands into his own and examined the mark we each had. A dragon in mid-flight glowed a soft white as he looked down at our hands.

"How long ago did this occur?" he asked, somehow maintaining the same tone as earlier, but conveying a heightened sense of concern. "When did you become Charkin?"

"A few weeks ago," I said, measuring my words carefully. I didn't know why he was agitated, and I didn't want to escalate the situation further. "We meant no offense."

"Offense?" he said, releasing our hands. "Quite the opposite. Char and her kin are welcome guests in my home. However, not everyone will hold you in such high esteem. For some, this is a mark of enmity. I would advise masking gloves in the future."

"Would that work?" I asked, looking down at the mark. "It gives off a particularly strong signature."

"On all except the most powerful, a masking glove should suffice," he said. "I'm certain your weaponsmith can create something suitable."

He possessed enough information to make me wary. The concern must have shown on my face because he smiled and motioned to the tea cups before taking his own and drinking.

"You are surprised I know of you and your organization?" he continued. "Yes?"

"Somewhat," I said. "We pride ourselves on keeping a low profile."

"It is not low enough," he said, glancing at Tiger. "For example, your second, Tiger, has made a name for herself, among allies and enemies alike, for her unrelenting ferocity and unshakeable fealty."

"It's a gift," Tiger said, glancing at me. "Ferocity and fealty fits."

"Likewise, the rest of your Directive is made up of some of the best," he continued. "Each excel in their specific disciplines. You have chosen well."

"Thank you," I said with a short nod. "It has not been easy."

He held up a finger.

"A wise leader is best when people barely know he exists," he said. "In this, you have failed."

"How so?" I asked as I felt Tiger slightly tense up beside me. "Would you be so kind as to explain?"

He nodded and took another sip from his tea. As he placed his cup down, he gazed at Tiger and then turned to stare at me.

"I shall speak plainly."

"We'd appreciate that, thanks," Tiger said. "Plain and simple works for me."

Altair smiled, but never took his eyes off of me.

"You cannot operate in the shadows when your very presence is a beacon of light," he said, pointing at the mark on my hand. "This is not a matter of hiding the mark. The Treadwell Supernatural Directive cannot hide for much longer."

"What does that mean?" Tiger said, keeping her voice calm as she looked down at her mark. "Is someone coming after us?"

"Not someone, something."

"Something?" she said.

"Isn't that why you are here?" Altair asked. "You want to know what organization would target you?"

"How did you—?" she started.

"A group like yours has no shortage of enemies," he said, focused on me. "Especially with your second's particular propensity for unleashing violence. Fear binds cowards and forces them into retaliation."

"You know about tonight's attack," I said. "How?"

He raised a hand and formed a small, blue flame in his palm. It danced in his hand, but gave off no heat. With a gesture of his fingers, it grew several times in size, the flame enveloping his entire hand, transforming into an orb of blazing heat.

He turned his hand over and shook it to the side, as if shaking the flame away. The blue orb sailed into the fireplace with a small explosion before disappearing.

"All runic flame is connected," he said, "even when it is corrupted and misused."

"You sensed the explosion earlier tonight?" Tiger asked. "From here?"

"If I had been in your position, I would have done the same," he said, ignoring Tiger's questions. "Especially when faced with a cinder cast."

"A cinder cast?" I asked. "What exactly is a cinder cast?"

"You faced a variation of one earlier this evening," he said. "It's a pyromantic cast designed to target and incinerate organic matter."

"That's exactly what we faced, except it was a bomb," Tiger said. "Two bombs attached to cars in fact. Do you know who could create something like that?"

"No, I don't," he said pensively. "Pyromancers do not congregate with each other often. Our personalities are too...volatile."

"I was told it was similar to a flashcast," I said. "Are you saying this is something else?"

"A flashcast is the lesser version of a cinder cast," he said. "In order to create a bomb, you would need a cinder cast and then you would inscribe it onto a device."

"How would it be triggered?" I asked. "Does it have a specific methodology?"

"The trigger would be specific to the pyromancer," he answered. "I don't know the specific trigger to the bomb you encountered."

"And you don't know *anyone* who could do this, really?" Tiger asked. "You are one of the most experienced pyromancers in the city."

"I am," Altair said, his voice becoming low and dangerous. "What are you insinuating?"

"That as the most experienced pyromancer, you might have *some* idea of who could pull off a cinder cast bomb," she said. "At the very least, you could point us in the right direction."

"Really?" he answered with a small smile. "How many kinetic mages inhabit this city? Do *you* have an accurate number?"

"No," Tiger admitted. "Kinetic mages are hard to track even when they are using their ability. We don't like drawing attention to ourselves."

He nodded.

"Then you understand my position," he said. "I am not Char. I do not broker in information, as valuable as it may be. I acquire and learn that which may be pertinent to me and my business. Outside of that purview, I do not make it a point to concern myself. I have, in fact, too much to deal with, with the Casbah; I've no time to keep track of renegade pyromancers out to eliminate you two."

"How advanced would a pyromancer need to be to create an explosive device with a cinder cast?" I asked. "Could you do it?"

"I could," he said pensively. "But I'm not particularly inclined to self-immolation for a bomb. Any pyromancer with the ability to wield a cinder cast would refuse. Unless..."

"Unless?" Tiger asked, keeping her voice calm. "Unless what?"

"You're looking for someone who has either recently shifted to a higher level and doesn't understand the danger of a cinder cast, or someone using a runic amplifier of some kind."

"A runic amplifier would allow for this?"

"With a gifted pyromancer, one who was hopelessly out of their depth, yes," he said. "They would be able to manage the cinder cast, without realizing the cost."

"The cost?" Tiger asked. "What is the cost?"

"All magic—energy manipulation, runic configuration, whatever name you choose to call it—has a cost, as you know," he said and formed a small orb of white flame in his hand as he answered. "Pyromancy has certain distinctions."

"Fire is a life-giver and life-taker," I said. "The cost is dual in nature?"

He looked at me and stared for a few seconds, before nodding approvingly and glancing at Tiger.

"I've heard some of the most advanced kinetic mages can use their own heartbeat to power their casts. Is this true?"

If there was one subject Tiger disliked discussing above all others, it was the subject of her abilities.

"The most advanced ones, the true masters, can use the

motion of quantum frequency," she answered, keeping her voice flat. "*Everything* has a frequency, even your thoughts."

"*That* in itself is a staggering concept," Altair said. "In pyromancy, there are many kinds of flame. Some can be harnessed for destruction, others for creation. The flame is neutral, indiscriminate. All that matters is how it's wielded."

"What is the consequence of using pyromancy for destruction?" I asked. "How does it exact its cost?"

"You said it earlier: life-giver and life-taker," he said. "A pyromancer abusing a destructive flame, like that of a cinder cast, is shortening their own life."

"You know," Tiger said, her voice low and full of menace. "You *know* who it can be."

"Tiger, what are you—?"

"He knows," she said, giving Altair a hard stare. "You can tell us who is using pyromancy this way."

"I may have an idea," he said, looking at Tiger. "Why should I help you?"

"Because to refuse means you're complicit with their actions," she answered. "Which means, if they tried to kill us, at the very least, you're okay with us being attacked. At worst, you're aligned with an enemy who wants us dead."

Altair closed his hand around the small orb and absorbed it.

"There is a third option," he said. "Would you like to hear it? Or do you think the real world only operates in black and white?"

"The real world only operates in black and shades of gray," she said. "There's darkness in everyone. The brighter the light, the deeper the shadow."

"And your light is so very bright," he said. "Your third option is this."

He reached out, and a channel of blue flame shot out

from his hand, ending at the sword over the fireplace. With a quick jerk of his hand, the Crimson Flame flew into his hand.

EIGHT

Altair drew the Crimson Flame and sliced down in one smooth motion, splitting the low table in two. I rolled back as Tiger dove to the side and threw up a wall of energy.

A moment later, the latent energy of the strike caused the table to explode into splinters as I moved back and jumped to my feet.

"We don't need to do this," I said, forming my blades. "Give us the information we need and we can walk away from this without spilling blood."

Altair stood slowly and shook his head.

"I cannot *give* you this information," he said. "This is all much deeper than you know, deeper than you could comprehend."

"I'm quite capable of profound comprehension."

"The situation you have stepped into is beyond you and your Directive."

With a small gesture, the blade of his sword was covered with blue flame as the silver blade turned a deep, blood red.

"Bloody hell," I muttered under my breath. "Why?"

"I will answer all your questions, if you manage to survive."

"And I don't manage to kill you."

"You are certainly welcome to try," he said with a small nod. "Stronger than you have tried...and failed."

"We're in your home," Tiger said. "What are you going to do, start throwing flame orbs around? You'll incinerate this place in seconds."

He formed an orb of blue flame and tossed it across the room. It hit the opposite wall and dissipated harmlessly, without leaving so much as a scorch mark. I had a feeling the effect would be radically different if that same orb hit one of us.

He was using cinder casts which would only burn organic matter.

"Fine, I didn't anticipate *that*," she said. "Those orbs are—"

"Cinder casts," I said, keeping my gaze on Altair. "Did *you* have a hand in creating those bombs?"

He thrust forward in response, nearly impaling me with his blade. I parried the thrust with my blades as he pushed me back. Tiger was staying back and waiting for an opening.

If she attacked, there was a good chance I would get caught in her cast. I needed to give her some space before she unleashed a kinetic attack.

Altair focused on me and flung an orb of blue flame at Tiger, who deflected it effortlessly with a wall of energy. The orb crashed into her wall and shattered into much smaller orbs which spread apart and tracked Tiger.

One of the orbs managed to get past her defenses, burning a hole in her arm. She glanced down at the wound and watched it heal, before she looked up at Altair.

"Sebastian, put him down, or I end him," she said, still

looking at Altair. "You're going to have to do better than that to stop me."

"I shall," Altair said, stepping back. "I only need to deal with one of you."

He slashed his blade horizontally in her direction, sending a wave of blue flame straight at her. She formed a wall of energy to intercept the flame of energy before it bisected her.

The flame crashed into her wall, releasing a burst of blue energy, flinging her back with force toward the far side of the room. She crashed into one of the bay windows, shattering it as her trajectory barely slowed. She flew out into the night, giving me one last glance before dropping out of sight.

We were on the ninth floor.

"A concussive scythe," he said, glancing at his flaming blade as he refocused on me. "A cast of my own making. It's quite effective against unconventional mages like your second. I'd like to extend my deepest condolences for her demise. Coming here was a fatal error on your part—another failure as a leader."

I remained silent for a few seconds and stared at him.

It was clear he was informed about me and the Directive, but the information he possessed was incomplete. If he thought a simple nine story drop was going to end Tiger, he was mistaken.

She would be back, and she would be livid when she returned.

"Your overconfidence will be your undoing," I said, making sure to keep the windows to my side. "You think *my* second would be so easy to defeat? To kill?"

"We're nine stories up," he said with a small smile. "Unless she has the power of flight, she is most certainly deceased."

I drew my blades up and stepped into a defensive stance.

"There's nothing more to say," I said. "Not with words, at least."

"Indeed," he said, sliding over to one side. "I will make this quick and merciful. Charkin deserve nothing less."

He stepped forward and led with a downward cut designed to cut across my chest. I stepped back away from the attack, as I unleashed my innersight. I read not only his energy signature, but his intentions. It allowed me to effectively predict his next move: a horizontal slash aimed at my legs.

I intercepted the slash with one of my blades before he could start, and sliced across his arm with the other. The cut wasn't deep, but it was deep enough. Energy flowed into me as my blade siphoned his power.

He stumbled back and disengaged as blue flame covered my blades.

"A siphon," he said surprised as he recovered. "I had no idea you wielded twin siphons. Impressive."

"There is much you don't know about me or the Directive."

"I know enough," he said, gathering himself but keeping his distance, "enough to end you."

I closed the distance as he readied his blade, holding it in front of his body diagonally. I *saw* the feint with my innersight as his energy signature shifted. I slid under the small, lethal barrage of blue orbs he unleashed in my direction.

I rolled to the side, rising next to him as I sliced through his unruned kimono and into his side. A grunt of pain escaped his lips as he swung his sword around, forcing me to duck and slice across one of his thighs.

More power flowed into me. The amount of energy was throwing me off as I stumbled back to deal with the influx of new power. I wasn't accustomed to wielding a siphon and the energy they transferred into me had transformed into a rush of vertigo and aggression as I adjusted to the unfamiliar sensation filling me.

He held his blade out between us as he grimaced and slid back, increasing the distance between us. He took several more steps back, gesturing as he covered his entire body in blue flame.

I understood in that moment how outclassed I was. If what he was using was a cinder cast, he had managed to sheathe himself in the deadly flames, yet remain unharmed.

I had never seen a pyromancer cover themselves in flame this way. He had effectively neutralized my preferred fighting distance. There was no way to get close to him now without suffering significant damage from the flames.

"You've never used a siphon," he said as the flames closed the wound in his side, stopping the bleeding. "It's too much power for you."

"I'll manage," I said and gritted my teeth. "It's only power."

"Power you're not accustomed to," he said. "You'll adjust eventually, but I won't give you that opportunity."

With blue flames covering his entire body, he rushed at me.

NINE

Several things happened next.

Altair lunged forward at me, sword first in an attempt to run his blade through my body. I stumbled back against a wall as I dealt with the energy of the siphon compromising my balance.

Then the front door to his home exploded in a chorus of screaming metal and shattered wood. Footsteps raced to my location, as an angry Tiger intercepted Altair mid-lunge, and drove a fist into his face, sending him back across the floor to land hard on his back.

Crimson Flame fell from his hand as he bounced several times on his way across the space. She closed the distance almost immediately, and I feared she had used her claws and killed him.

The absence of blood covering the floor indicated otherwise, but if she had hardened her fist, she could have just as easily crushed his skull with that blow. When he slid to a stop, she stood over him, aiming a very large gun into his face.

He didn't move.

The fact that she was still aiming the Eradicator at him led me to believe she had shown considerable restraint and left him alive. I stared in mild shock as his rising and falling chest confirmed my thoughts.

"I didn't kill him," she said with a growl. "Though I should have."

"That is what I call restraint. Well done. Wake him up."

"What happened to you?" she said, giving me a quick glance. "You look like hell. What's wrong? Don't tell me he had you on your heels?"

"No. The siphon," I said, holding up a blade by way of explanation. "Still dealing with the energy transfer. Not...not used to his energy."

She nodded.

"You're going to have to practice with those things," she said, looking down at Altair. "You sure you want him conscious? He's bound to try something stupid and life-shortening."

I gestured and formed an orb of blue flame.

"I think we can deter him from making a poor life choice," I said, nodding at her. "Let's get some answers."

"I just want to know if I can—"

"No," I said, knowing where she was going with this. "You cannot throw him out of the window when we're done. He's an acquaintance of Char; we will extend the courtesy of letting him live, out of deference to her."

"Fine," she grumbled. "But if he so much as twitches the wrong way, I'm eradicating his head from his shoulders."

"Duly noted," I managed as nausea gripped me, forcing me to lean against a wall again before I crossed the floor. "This will take some getting used to. Wake him up. I have questions."

She gestured and unleashed a small amount of power, slowly slapping him in the face with a kinetic cast. He groaned in pain as Tiger continued her not-so-gentle resuscitation technique of slapping him awake.

I paused to pick up Crimson Flame to prevent him from calling it to his hand again, as I made my way to where she stood. Altair slowly regained consciousness and tried to slide away from Tiger, who shook her head, aiming the Eradicator at his head.

He sat against the wall and stared at her.

"I'm going to explain this once so I don't have to waste time repeating myself," she said. "Do you see your door?"

She pointed down the corridor which ended at the front door—which was currently missing.

"What front door?" Altair answered, upset. "You destroyed it."

"Exactly. I just blew through your door and defenses with this thing," she said, keeping her voice soft as she glanced at the Eradicator. "Imagine what I could do to your head at point-blank range."

"The same thing you did to my door, I would imagine."

"You imagine correctly," she answered. "I so much as feel a one degree temperature rise, or see any flame of any kind, and you will lose your head, figuratively and literally. Clear?"

"Absolutely," he said, looking down the barrel of the Eradicator. "You are more resilient than I expected. I underestimated you both."

"We get that often," she said and glanced my way. "Ask away."

I stepped forward to the fireplace and sheathed Crimson Flame in its saya before removing it from the fireplace. Then I turned to face Altair, still holding his sword.

"Who runs Maledicta and how did they create the cinder cast?"

Altair smiled and nodded.

"How did you know?" Altair asked as he leaned against the wall. "Char did say you had a keen intelligence."

"Know? Know what?" Tiger asked. "What did he know? What's going on?"

"He was prepared to answer our questions," I said, looking at Altair. "But it was conditional."

"It had to be," he said, raising a hand as Tiger glared at him. "If you couldn't deal with facing me, then sending you to Maledicta would have been a death sentence. I would not have your blood on my hands. Char would never forgive me for that."

"But she's okay with you blasting me out of a window and trying to slice and flambé us?" Tiger asked, still pointing the Eradicator at Altair. "That she's okay with?"

"You are Charkin," Altair said as if that explained it all. "She does not give her mark easily or to those who she deems unworthy. If you wear her mark, you must be formidable. I am, however, surprised you survived the fall. How did you do it?"

"We're asking the questions," Tiger said.

"You assumed we were formidable, but you had to make sure," I said. "Why?"

"Because the leadership of Maledicta has recently shifted in power," he said. "It has increased exponentially in a short span of time. Too short a span for such an increase in power."

"Powerful enough to create the cinder cast bombs," I said. "Cinder casts that could destroy organic targets."

"Powerful enough for me to sense a detonation on the FDR from here," he said, his expression dark. "The amount of power required to expend that much energy is staggering."

"No one in Maledicta possesses that much power?" I asked. "Are you saying that shouldn't have been possible?"

"No, it shouldn't have," he said, staring at Tiger. "Would

you mind putting that thing away? I'm not going to attack you again."

Tiger looked at me and I gave her a slight nod.

"I'm going to stop pointing it at you," she said, lowering the weapon. "Don't give me another reason to shoot you."

"Another reason?" he asked. "What reason—"

"Nine story drop to the street below," Tiger said, cutting him off. "Do I need to say more?"

"No," he said with a nod. "Would you tell me how you did it? You're only a kinetic mage. I didn't think you were advanced enough to survive that fall."

"So you felt the need to test the theory?"

"I felt the need to test if you had earned the privilege of being Charkin."

"You could have asked," she said as the anger rose in her voice. "What would you have done if I hadn't survived?"

"Reparations to Char in whatever way she deemed fit," he said. "It wasn't personal."

"Not personal?" she said with a smile. "It felt fairly personal as I dropped to the street."

"Taking it personally would be an error on your part," he said, endangering his life further. "Getting emotional over my actions would only confirm your immaturity."

She glanced at me and I gave her a look that let her know not to do whatever it was she was thinking.

"I have a question for you," she said. "Could you survive a nine story fall?"

"Yes," he said foolishly and I sighed. "It would be child's play. I am an accomplished pyromancer and can manipul—"

She grabbed him by the kimono, lifting him up off his feet, and stared into his face. He was surprised, shocked, and angry all at once.

Part of what made her so dangerous was her unnatural strength. She was deceptively strong for her stature.

"Being the mature pyromancer I know you are," she said, staring up into his enraged face, "I know you won't take this personally."

"I won't take what personally?" he demanded. "Unhand me."

"I will, in a second."

She tightened her grip on him, rotated her torso as she bent over, and took two large steps forward, doing her best impression of a shot putter. On the second to last rotation, she let go and Altair became airborne.

Thankfully, she aimed for the window she had shattered, sparing him the impact and additional injuries of crashing through a window.

With one smooth motion, she had flung him out of his home and into the night.

TEN

"What?" she said as I stared at her. "He said he could survive it. Either he was lying, or he will be here in a few minutes."

"I truly hope you didn't kill him," I said, walking over to the window and peering down to the street. "He's not down there, so it seems he was being truthful."

"See?" she said. "Let's see if he's eager to answer questions about how he did it when he gets back here."

I looked down at the sword I held.

It was the perfect metaphor for my relationship with Tiger.

"That was *not* restraint," I said after a moment. "You do not need to act on every impulse you have. At least not immediately, and especially not on the violent ones."

"You think I acted rashly?"

"Rashly would have been breaking some bones," I said. "You jettisoned him from his home."

"The same way he tossed me out of his window," she said. "Do you think he acted rashly?"

"No," I said, shaking my head. "He was certifiable, just for attempting to hurt you with this sword. It was obvious from his behavior that he wasn't aware of your capacity for violence."

"True," she said, giving it some thought. "Most people who know me, or know of me, wouldn't have opted to throw me out of a window without expecting me to retaliate. You think he was given bad information about us?"

"Maybe not bad, but certainly incomplete," I said "Had he known more, he wouldn't have taken his life into his hands that way. You, on the other hand, could have resisted your first impulse and not thrown him out of said window."

"That wasn't my first impulse."

"No? Do I even want to know?"

"My *first* impulse was to separate his torso from the rest of his body," she said, menace lacing her voice as she glanced at the window that had become an impromptu exit for Altair. "I managed to restrain myself from doing that. Then, I exercised more restraint, stopping myself from burying my claws into his face. I'd say this was a major restraint moment, considering the situation."

"Agreed," I admitted. "Have you gotten it out of your system?"

"Gotten *what* out of my system?"

"Your immediate rage and desire for retribution," I said, realizing my error the moment the words escaped my lips. "I mean—"

"My *rage*, is not caused by some self-important pyromancer hiding out in his gilded cage of a home," she said, cutting me off. "My rage is an ever-present part of me, and you, of all people, know this. I can't believe you even had to ask."

"My apologies, it appears the earlier siphoning has addled my senses," I said. "Can I speak to him without the threat of his imminent demise?"

"That depends on him," she said as I heard footsteps at

the doorway. Altair stepped into the living room, a dark and dangerous expression on his face. She turned to face him with a smile on her face. "Altair, welcome back. You survived...how *did* you do it?"

"Tiger..." I warned, watching the anger seethe in his face. "Let it go."

"I did," she answered. "Ask him what you need to know, so we can get out of here. Next time, I won't be so *restrained*."

Altair made his way slowly to a zabuton and sat down. I could tell he was still rattled by his sudden departure from the living room to the street below.

"Tell me about Maledicta," I said. "Who currently leads them?"

He stared at Tiger.

"You threw me out of a window," he said, ignoring me. "We're nine stories up. You could have killed me."

"Not as exhilarating when *you're* the one being thrown out of the window, is it?"

"I can't believe you would—"

Tiger gave me a look and turned to exit the living room.

"I'll wait for you in the Tank," she said, cutting him off as she paused to glance at Altair one last time. "If I stay here, things *will* get personal."

She grabbed her shoes and left.

"She's insane," he said when he was sure she was out of earshot. "Why do you associate with such violence?"

"Violence is the currency and language of this life we live," I said. "She just happens to be quite fluent and wealthy in it."

"Your second is going to get you killed one day," he said, looking at what remained of his door. "I can't believe she's roaming the streets free."

"Like you said earlier, she possesses unrelenting ferocity," I said, placing the Crimson Flame in its display stand over the fireplace. "She is feared and respected because she is capable of mind-numbing violence. Most mistake her appearance for weakness. It's a mistake made once. As for why I associate with her, she's my family."

"You made her your second," he countered. "Your wisdom in this matter is questionable at best, and deranged at worst. You must see what an error that is. She is a volatile and dangerous variable, jeopardizing any dealings you may have."

I paused a moment and turned to take in the view, which was quite impressive as the sun lightened the sky with the approaching dawn.

Unlike Tiger, I couldn't reflexively bury a blade in his neck and end his existence. Actually, I could, but I feared that would truly unleash the violence inside of Tiger.

The rage that roiled within me made Tiger's ever-present anger look like a child's tantrum. I couldn't afford to lose control of it...ever. If I did, there was a strong possibility that my uncle Dexter would pay me a short and cataclysmic visit, cutting my life expectancy short.

I took a deep breath, remained calm, and re-examined Altair. He was the product of an entitled life, an elitism born out of a sheltered existence within the upper echelons of the magical community.

His arrogance wasn't born from battle.

I doubted he had ever had to fight for his life on the streets of this or any city. His hubris stemmed from moving in the exclusive circles of privilege and excess, where actions had little to no consequence.

It was true he had skill.

His ability as a pyromancer was quite advanced, as was his business acumen, considering his accomplishments with the Casbah. But all of that paled in comparison when faced with someone like Tiger.

He was operating by some mythological rules of conduct that didn't exist in Tiger's or my world. Frankly, they didn't exist in his world either, except that he had been used to having a buffer of privilege between him and true violence for so long that he had been lulled into thinking it didn't exist.

He was wrong.

Tonight, that buffer had been ripped away, exposing him to reality for what was perhaps the first time in his life. There was only one rule that governed Tiger's behavior—*There are no rules.*

I took another deep breath and let it out slowly.

"I made her my second"—another slight pause—"because she is the best at what she does and who she is. There is no one else on the face of this planet I would want by my side if I was headed into battle. Not only is she exceptional as a fighter, she is a gifted tactician, and in my absence, is more than capable to oversee the Directive."

"I see," he said. "My apologies, I misspoke. I am certain you have your reasons, even if they currently escape me. I am certain Lady Char would not miscalculate in giving you or your second her mark. Please, sit."

I sat opposite him and glanced out of the window for a moment.

"You have my apologies for any damage caused to your home," I said. "It was not my intention to disrupt your life, nor bring chaos to your home. Please allow me to defray any of the costs incurred tonight."

"Unnecessary," he said, gazing out of the broken window. "Any damage incurred was due to my negligence."

"I must insist," I said, knowing this game well as I handed him a card. "Please have your people contact the Directive; we will take care of the damages."

"Char's confidence in you is well placed," he said, taking the card and waving my words away. "Do not concern yourself with that which can be replaced. Today, with your words and acts, you have made an ally."

I filed the words away for future reference. Allies of fear and convenience usually became enemies born from cowardice and pressure when the situation shifted in their favor.

"I am grateful to hear that," I said. "What can you tell me about Maledicta?"

"An organization of dark mage assassins, they have recently risen to prominence," he said, staring at me before pouring himself more tea. "I hear that is partly due to your actions?"

"I have had no interaction with Maledicta, at least not knowingly," I said, confused. "I do not work with dark mage assassins, nor do I hire them to work for me."

It was his turn to pause.

"Perhaps not directly, no," he said. "But with Umbra's demise as an organization, Maledicta stepped into the void created by their absence. You *did* play an active role in Umbra's dissolution, did you not?"

"I did," I said, measuring my words carefully. "It could not be helped."

"You will face no recriminations from me," he said. "Umbra was a blight on the city and needed to be eliminated."

"You don't believe the same about Maledicta?"

"Maledicta provides a necessary service," he said, "one that is utilized by many powerful individuals in this city. Those individuals would take it as a personal affront if you choose to oppose them or destroy Maledicta."

"I see."

"More than most, according to my information," he said, "you will have to proceed with utmost caution. If you face off against Maledicta, you can easily find yourself facing a war on several fronts—a war you cannot win."

"I will take that into consideration," I said. "This sudden power surge you mentioned earlier, do you know its source?"

"There have been rumors of a gem—a sacred amethyst that has been recently acquired," he said. "But Maledicta has gone silent as of late. This most recent attack on you has all the indications of the group, but if it had been a true reprisal, we would not be having this conversation right now. You and your Directive would be dead."

I didn't bother to argue the point that we weren't that easy to kill.

"Two more things: how long ago did they go silent, and when did Maledicta start rising to prominence?"

"They've been silent for close to two weeks and only recently have been rising to prominence—well, as much prominence as a group of dark mage assassins would embrace," he said. "They are establishing themselves in subtle, violent ways."

"More deaths?"

"You could say their services have been utilized more frequently in the last few weeks," he replied. "Their method of execution is quite unique. They don't use car bombs."

"You're saying it wasn't Maledicta?" I asked. "Then who attempted to kill us earlier?"

"Prior to the attack, were you asking about Maledicta?"

"Yes."

"Then more than likely it was a fringe group designated as a trigger response to your inquiries," he said. "Had it been the true organization, you would still be either fighting, or fleeing for your life, at this very moment."

"Dark mage assassins don't blow up cars?"

"Dark mage assassins don't fail," he answered. "There is a reason Maledicta is feared. If they accept a contract, they fulfill it. Even if it means their death, failure is never an option. Did you ask about the gem?"

"Yes," I said, being cautious with the information I gave him. He may have declared us allies, but he had tried to skewer me several times this evening. I'd consider us distant acquaintances at best. "We are looking into the sacred amethyst."

"Why?"

"A favor for a friend," I said, which was partially true. "I need to find it."

"A favor like this could prove fatal—for you and the Directive."

"I'm aware," I said, becoming more aware every second that my blood debt with Heka and the Wordweavers was turning into something larger than I'd bargained for. "I still need to find it."

"Need or want?"

"Excuse me?"

"You said you *need* to find it," he said. "Do you need to find it, or do you want to find it?"

"Need to," I said. "That amethyst possesses some dangerous properties. I need to return it to its rightful owner."

"Is this amethyst an amplifier?" he asked. "It's the only explanation for the increase in power in Maledicta's leadership."

I paused again and he nodded.

"Your silence speaks louder than any words," he continued. "It would be safe to say that this amplifier has fallen into the hands of Maledicta. The leader is a gifted pyromancer, but not so gifted that he could unleash a cinder cast on his own."

"Unless he had an amplifier," I said. "Is he as gifted as you?"

"I'm not gifted, I'm old," he said. "There's a difference. I'm old enough to stay away from an amplifier of this sort.

Knowledge makes you humble; arrogance makes one igno-
rant, and none are more arrogant than the young."

"How do I locate the actual organization? Who leads it?"

He took another, longer sip from his cup.

"Once I share this information with you, we will not
speak again," he said. "If this matter is resolved, and you
survive, I will have more to share with you. If not, this will be
our final conversation. Are we in agreement?"

I didn't have much of a choice. I needed the information
he had.

"Yes," I said. "I free you from any obligation you may have
to share the knowledge you possess, until after this matter is
resolved and only if I, or my second, have survived. If we fall,
the obligation placed on you is null and void."

"Very well," he said, agreeing to my slightly amended
agreement. "If either of you survive your encounter, we will
speak again. The person you are looking for is Calum Kers.
He is the current leader of Maledicta and has recently shifted
in power."

"Where do I find him?"

"Where you always find the most dangerous assassins...in
the shadows."

ELEVEN

I exited Phoenix Hall and paused at the entrance to look up the nine stories, both Tiger and Altair had fallen. I had an idea how Altair had managed to save himself from a gruesome fate. Pyromancers could use their ability to create a cushion of superheated air and slow the fall to a soft drop.

Tiger's solution would be riskier.

She would need to create several platforms of energy, using each one as a barrier to slow her descent to the street as she fell. If she didn't have the ability to harden her skin, she would break multiple bones on her way down.

Of course, the alternative was breaking everything when she landed. It was no small wonder she was livid at being thrown out of the window. The fact that Altair was still breathing unassisted still amazed me.

With a shake of my head, I headed to the Tank and reviewed what Altair had shared with me.

We had a target.

Calum Kers.

There were several problems with this information.

First, I didn't know who this Calum Kers was. That in

itself wasn't alarming; I didn't keep track of every dark mage assassin in the city. What concerned me was that Honor had recently shared the same thing about the assassin group.

Maledicta had recently gone dark.

Why would they opt to disappear? Aside from the usual, dark mage assassins keeping a low to invisible profile, this was something more, and I had a feeling it had something to do with the amethyst.

And Regina.

I still remembered her words when we spoke last:

You know why I'm here.

They're not going to give it to you.

I'm not asking.

If she managed to get her hands on the sacred amethyst, this situation would go from bad to hellish in the space of a heartbeat. I couldn't let her get her hands on the amethyst.

If I was being honest, I knew it was coming to this the moment she set foot in the city. Sooner or later she was going to attempt something dangerous and foolish and I was going to have to do something even more dangerous and foolish...I was going to have to stop her.

I entered the Tank on the passenger side and strapped in. Tiger gave me an expectant look as she turned on the engine.

The deep throaty rumble washed over us as the Tank flexed its automotive muscle. There was no mistaking the sound of its engine as it growled into the night, threatening any who dared to step near.

There were times when I wondered what kind of ability Cecil and his people at SuNaTran possessed that allowed them to work their particular automancy, making their vehicles feel alive and actually menacing.

"Well?" she asked, lightly stepping on the accelerator and most likely waking up all of Gramercy Park at this hour. "What did he say? Do I need to go back up there?"

I glanced at the front of the Hall.

The last thing I needed was Tiger paying Altair another visit. I had a strong suspicion that another visit would prove lethal...for him.

"I think Altair has had enough near-death experiences for one evening."

"One quick visit would do him some good," she said. "Teach him not to throw guests out of his windows. Where I come from that's considered rude."

"Really? Where you come from they actually have a protocol for window egress?"

"Where I come from, if you throw someone out of a window you better make sure its high enough that they don't survive the fall," she said. "And if they do, you better be prepared to convince them that they should have chosen not to survive the fall."

"Regarding that, why *did* you go back up?" I said. "You could have stayed down here in the Tank, but you chose to return. Were you concerned about my well-being? Did you really think I was in danger?"

"You *were* in danger," she corrected. "When I got back up there, you were drunk off your ass with the power you had siphoned."

"I was completely in control," I protested. "In fact, I was—"

"About to get shish kebabed with that sword of his," she finished. "But that wasn't the reason I went back up there."

"You were upset," I said. "He did throw you out of a window. I can understand your anger. Frankly, I'm surprised you only returned the favor. You've done worse for less. It really is a—"

"Are you done?" she asked, giving me a look. "Yes, I was upset, but that's not why I went back up."

"You *were* concerned for me," I said with a nod. "I do appreciate that."

She sighed and pointed down at her feet.

"No, I went back for my Bifrosts," she said. "They were still up there when he threw me out of the window, and I knew you would forget them. Do you know how much they cost?"

I gave her a withering glare.

"No, but I have a feeling you're going to tell me."

"Retail, they're insanely expensive," she said. "Having Christian attend to me personally while they were fabricated makes them priceless. He would be livid if I lost them."

"We wouldn't want Christian upset at you now."

"First thing you said tonight that makes sense," she said. "I do not want my very exclusive and gifted shoe designer upset with me. *You* don't want my designer upset with me, either."

"I don't'?"

"If he's upset with me, then I'm upset, period. That makes me unpleasant to be around," she said with a straight face. "I find it difficult to find my tranquil and balanced center when I'm upset."

"You strung some sentences together there, that defy explanation in regards to you and your disposition," I said. "Starting with tranquil and balanced center."

"I *am* tranquil and balanced. That's why Altair is still alive."

"I can't believe you went back for some shoes," I said in disbelief. "I was in mortal danger."

"You were never in *mortal* danger," she said. "These are not just *some shoes*. These are my Louboutin Bifrosts. They are impossible to get anywhere else, but Paris."

"Shoes," I repeated, shaking my head. "You went back for *shoes?*"

"Drop it," she warned. "What else did he say?"

I dropped it because as much as she loved her shoes, she was slightly touchy on the subject. I briefed her on what Altair had shared with me.

"You're thinking this Calum has the sacred amethyst?"

"It makes the most sense," I said, pulling out my phone and calling the Church. "We need more information on him and this group."

"What about your woman?" Tiger asked. "You know she's going to go for it. She said as much the last time we saw her. She's a credible threat, one we can't ignore."

"She's not my wo—"

"Denial is not a good look on you," Tiger said, cutting me off. "I may not respect her as a person, but I respect the threat she poses. Her skill as a blademaster and thief makes her dangerous. If she wants that gem, we're probably the only ones who know how she operates. Maledicta won't stand a chance against her, even if they are dark mage assassins. We have to stop her."

"Stop, not kill."

She shrugged her shoulders.

"Regina isn't big on restraint, last I recall," Tiger said, her voice low and dark. "If she hands it over without trying to take us out, I'd call that a win. We all get to walk away."

"And if she doesn't hand it over?"

"We both know she's not just going to hand it over," Tiger answered. "When she tries to turn me into a pincushion with those blades of hers, I'm not going to stand there and smile at her. I will end her."

"You will try."

"I live for the small pleasures in life," she said with a dangerous smile. "We all know she will unleash her blades on us, well, almost all of us know this. There are some deluded mages who believe in love. Those usually end up with a blade in their heart."

"She does have a way of making a point."

"Usually to the hilt."

She was right.

The odds of Regina giving up the sacred amethyst without conflict, especially if it was an artifact of power, were slim to non-existent. Knowing Regina, she had several buyers lined up, and she would sell the amethyst to the highest bidder.

She never kept the artifacts she *liberated*.

"Calum is a gifted pyromancer. If he has the amethyst, it's made him a menace we need to stop," I said. "Regina will have her hands full getting it from him."

"I'm pretty sure he was a menace before he got the gem," she said. "We need to get it before Regina does."

"We will, once we find Maledicta and Calum."

"Do you think that's who Amina gave the gem to?"

"I don't think she knew who she gave the gem to," I said. "She was just making a delivery. I doubt this Calum would meet with her. I am surprised, however, that he left her alive."

"True," she said. "That was either sloppy, devious, or careful. Not a good policy to kill a Wordweaver. Even one that's betraying her sisters."

"Why devious though?" I said as the call connected and diverted my attention. "You'll have to explain that."

"Treadwell Supernatural Directive," Rabbit said. "We walk the shadows, so you can enjoy the light. How may I direct your call?"

"You know it's me, Rabbit. Is Rat in?"

"He is," she said, maintaining her receptionist voice. "We have to uphold a certain level of professionalism around here, you know. Would you like to be connected?"

"I would," I said, keeping my voice even. "Have you made any progress on finding the new receptionist? A real one?"

"I have a few candidates," she said. "Sadly, some crashed and burned during the extensive interview process, but I have a few more who look promising."

I pinched the bridge of my nose to stave off the impending headache. Rabbit may have been acting as the temporary receptionist, but her real skill was being a skilled counterintelligence asset, who usually worked missions together with Rat.

Whatever she was having the candidates do as part of her extensive interview process, I was certain it violated several laws in several countries.

"Do I want to know what this interview process entails?" I asked. "Or am I going to get a call from INTERPOL's Dark Division?"

INTERPOL was known around the world as the International Criminal Police Organization. Within the larger body of the organization was the Dark Division.

The IDD were the ones who dealt with the supernatural threats without needing to follow any kind of supernatural due process. These were the people who showed up in the middle of the night and disappeared targets.

No one voluntarily picked a fight with the IDD or their Director, Rose Brock. She was about as pleasant as a troll fist to the face. In fact, if I had to choose, the troll fist would win every single time.

Brock was dangerous, intelligent, ruthless, and unwavering when she pursued a target. The best course of action when dealing with the IDD, was not to deal with them at all. Staying off their radar was always the best strategy.

The IDD was a bear no one in the supernatural community poked. Even Char gave them a wide berth and to my knowledge, Char feared nothing and no one. Yet even she respected the world of pain the IDD could unleash.

We had poked the IDD a few times in the past, and it had never ended well. As far as I knew, we were on their watch list for subversive, radical, and criminal supernatural behavior. A status I think all the members of the Directive were secretly proud to hold.

All the members except me, that is.

"No need to drag IDD into any of this," she said quickly. "I'm keeping all of these interviews mostly above board."

"Mostly?"

"It's legal, well, mostly legal, and I have them sign a waiver too," she said. "Don't worry, Boss. I'm sure we'll find a receptionist soon."

"I'm not worried," I said, worried she may be sending these candidates to Haven or worse. "I'm sure you will do your best. Rat, please."

"I'll connect you to his lab, one second."

The line went silent as the Tank rumbled again.

The low rumble vibrated through my body as Tiger pulled away from Phoenix Hall. She glanced back at the building once before leaving the Gramercy Park area.

"Ox briefed me on the attack earlier," Rat said as he came on the line. "I don't have much information on the car bombs, but the casts were some type of pyromancy which targeted only the victims."

"Cinder casts," I said. "I was told they require a high degree of skill to cast and create."

"I'll look into it, but that's not why you're calling," he said. "You want to know who's behind the attack."

"Yes, but there's someone else I need you to look into first," I said, marveling at how he always knew what I wanted when I called. "I need to know where this group, Maledicta, is headquartered, and who is Calum Kers. Apparently, he's currently leading them."

"Calum Kers?" he said after a pause. "Are you certain that was the name you were given?"

"You know him?"

"I know *of* him, and none of it is good," he said. "Dark mage assassins with a reputation for fulfilling their contracts. They have a ninety-five percent completion rate."

"Ninety-five?" I asked, surprised at the high rate. "What happened to the other five percent?"

"Voluntary cancellations, which are covered by their unique reparation clause," Rat said. "If they fail a contract, or cancel it for any reason, the client is returned the hiring fee, plus a percentage, for inconvenience."

"I've never heard of that," I said. "Why would they cancel a contract?"

"A few reasons, unforeseen variables, heightened difficulty, or death of the assassin assigned to the contract," Rat said in his soft, methodical voice. "It doesn't happen often; Male-dicta is one of the best conflict resolution firms in existence."

"Conflict resolution?" I asked. "Is that what we're calling a house of assassins these days?"

"It's what they're hired to do," he said. "They get paid to make conflicts disappear, thus resolving them."

"Understood. How long has Calum led Maledicta?"

"Two years," Rat said. "He killed his way up the ranks, which is the typical method of promotion in a group like Maledicta. He was more ruthless than most and ascended faster because of it."

"He is a gifted pyromancer," I said. "At least that is what I was informed."

"By whom?"

"Altair."

"The source is less than reliable, but the information is

solid," Rat confirmed. "Calum is a considerable pyromantic threat; his presence is what keeps the dark mages of Maledicta pliant."

"Put a file together on him."

"I already have," he said. "I'll send over what I have. Finding their headquarters will take some digging. They like to keep a lower profile than most. Once I have actionable information, I'll send that over as well."

"We need to find him," I said, thinking over options. "He may be in possession of a powerful artifact."

"Which is?"

"A sacred amethyst which can cause a sudden shift in power in the mage that possesses it," I said. "Something like that in Calum's hands—"

"Would be detrimental," he said and paused again. I knew he was making mental connections and waited until he came to a conclusion. "Is this the same sacred amethyst stolen from the Wordweavers?"

"Yes," I said. "I need to retrieve it for Heka."

"You *are* aware Regina Clark is in the city?"

"I'm aware."

"We can safely extrapolate that she will be in pursuit of this amethyst," he said. "Do you have contingency plans in place?"

"The plan is simple: find Calum, get the gem before she does."

"It never goes quite that simply and Ms. Clark is a formidable variable."

"That's one way of describing her," I said. "We can't let her get that gem."

"Understood, there may be another method to use here," Rat said after another pause, "if you're open to an unconventional method."

"What unconventional method?"

"I have people on Ms. Clark," Rat said. "There is a good chance she will make a play for Calum, or more precisely the gem he holds."

"You want to intercept her before she gets to Calum?"

"Before she gets to the gem," he said. "She can lead us to both, Calum and the gem."

"You're proposing using her as bait?"

"Not bait," Rat answered. "More like a pathfinder. She can point us in the right direction."

"She won't be satisfied with merely pointing the direction," I said. "Once she knows where he is, she will act, and fast."

"We will have to act first," Rat said. "Her acquisition of the gem is a non-option."

"I like this plan," Tiger said, heading downtown. "It should keep her distracted, and we move in before she gets the amethyst. She may accidentally get caught in some crossfire. *That* would be a pity."

"This is Regina," I said. "By now, she most likely knows Rat has people on her. Don't forget, the same way we know how she operates, she knows how we operate."

"There is that risk," Rat said. "How would you like me to proceed?"

"Keep your people on her, but rotate them regularly," I said. "Don't let her see the same face twice. Keep me in the loop. When you think she is on approach to Calum and the gem, we'll make our move."

"I have a contact inside Maledicta," Rat said. "If I can reach out to her without arousing suspicion, I'll utilize her assistance."

"You have a contact inside Maledicta?"

"I have contacts inside almost everywhere," he said. "She's not an asset and she doesn't know who I am. Everything she does is tangentially beneficial to what we need."

"I'm still trying to understand how you have a contact inside Maledicta," Tiger said. "How did you do that?"

"Trade secrets," he said. "Once I know more, I'll inform you both."

"I appreciate it," I said. "One more thing—do you and Calum have history?"

"Yes," he said after a pause. "Some of it good, most of it lethal."

He ended the call.

"What was that?" Tiger said. "I've never heard Rat hesitate."

"You noticed that," I said, thinking the same thing. "It seems the history Rat and Calum have predates the Directive."

"Do you think it will affect him?" she asked. "Rat usually plays everything close to the chest. You know him better than everyone except maybe Rabbit."

"Rat is a professional," I said. "He'll do what he needs to do to fulfill the mission. More than that though, I trust him. If this history between him and Calum will be a problem, or prevent him from carrying out his duties, I'm certain he'll let me know."

She nodded.

"Where to?" she asked. "Breakfast?"

"After this evening's events, I could eat."

"Where?"

"Let's go to the deli," I said. "It's the only place I can get a decent English Breakfast in this city."

"You sure," she asked, swerving around traffic. "You know it's not the place, but the clientele that concerns me."

"I doubt the clientele would try anything inside the walls of the deli."

"It's not inside the walls of the deli that I'm thinking

about," she said. "The last time we were there, those ogres followed us for five blocks before making a move."

"Which you promptly neutralized."

"I just want breakfast, not breakfast and a battle, just breakfast," she said. "Is that too much to ask?"

"I'll have a word with Ezra," I said. "He's usually very persuasive in these matters."

TWELVE

We arrived downtown as Tiger parked the Tank across the street from Ezra's establishment.

The morning sun blazed across the horizon as we exited the vehicle. I placed a hand on the surface of the Tank, causing the locking runes to activate with an orange shimmer and a deep *clang* of metal on metal.

Tiger stood motionless for a few moments and stared across the street.

It wasn't that she disliked Ezra—she actually liked the old scholar—but Tiger was peculiar about what Ezra represented. She had difficulty reconciling that Ezra was the personification of Death.

"Are you okay?" I asked as she stared across the street. "Would you prefer to go elsewhere?"

"Ezra has some of, if not the best pastrami sandwiches in the city," she said with a small shake of her head. "I'm not passing that up just because he's Death. We've faced worse for less."

"True," I said as we crossed the street. "Just making sure you're good with this. I know how you feel about him."

"I'm not good with this," she said, glaring at traffic as we crossed, forcing drivers to either stop or swerve around us as we navigated E. Houston Street in our typical fashion, which was a cross between traversing the wide street and suicide. "But I'm not going to let a little thing like facing off against the Scholar of Death stop me from my pastrami."

"Does he know you call him that?"

"Do you really think anything escapes him?" she asked as we sprinted across the street, avoiding a truck followed by a yellow taxi determined to make the light, even if it meant reducing us to paste in the process. "He pretty much sees everything, don't you think?"

"Are you asking me if Death or this personification of death is omniscient?" I answered, giving the question thought. "I don't know if he sees everything; Ezra has never explained how he does what he does, to me. Though to be honest, I've never really asked."

"I think he already knows," she said as we approached the entrance to the deli. "He may not know everything—even though I think he does—but nothing escapes him. He's Death after all."

"A concept we are both intimately familiar with, but a rabbit hole I have no desire of falling into," I said as we crossed the threshold. "Ezra is an unknown I prefer remain that way until I need to have my final conversation with him."

"Death is not the issue," she said. "We all have to meet it or him, someday. For me, it's the living that's difficult."

The runes along the threshold flared orange as we entered the deli. A frisson of energy crossed over my skin as we stepped into Ezra's establishment. The interior was a duplicate of Katz's Deli and it was my understanding that Ezra's was the supernatural equivalent of the same, except that it occupied a tangential space in an adjacent plane.

At the entrance, the two places overlapped briefly,

creating a paradox of sorts, allowing for the normal clientele to enter Katz's, while the supernatural customers entered Ezra's.

As far as neutral locations went, Ezra's was the most secure and known in the city. No one willfully violated the space with violence, and even beings on Char's level of power observed a policy of strict neutrality when they visited.

I hesitated a moment at the doorway as Tiger continued inside. I took a moment to gaze inside and assess the potential threats we would be facing.

I sensed a slight ripple of energy flow around the space as Tiger kept walking. I focused my peripheral attention in the direction of the fluctuation and scanned the area.

There were several individuals with considerable energy signatures, but nothing too out of the ordinary, until I turned to gaze into a far corner. There, sat a man doing his best to blend in by suppressing his substantial signature.

Anyone going through that much trouble was hiding from someone or something. I made a mental note of the person and kept walking, following Tiger over to another corner where Ezra usually sat.

I managed to catch up to Tiger before we reached Ezra.

"We may have a problem," I said under my breath as I drew up next to her. "Far corner to the right. Recognize the signature?"

She kept walking, but let her senses expand.

"Shit," she said in the same tone I had used. "Is that Uluru? It can't be. I heard he was retired abroad."

"Seems he's back."

"Coincidence?" she asked. "Could be he's here for a hearty breakfast too."

"You know I don't believe in coincidence," I said as we drew closer to Ezra's table. "Uluru's presence here could be happenstance, but how often does that happen in our lives?"

"Never," she said. "Breakfast before battle. I'm serious. It's not like he's going to try anything in here anyway."

"True," I said. "Let's not keep our host waiting."

Ezra was, as usual, examining some large tome; the title was currently hidden from view, but I was certain he would share it with me momentarily. Ezra enjoyed showing off his books—the more obscure the better.

The seats around his table were empty. No one approached his table uninvited, unless they truly possessed a desire to dramatically shorten their lives.

He wore his usual pair of half-moon glasses, and peered over at me for a few seconds as we crossed the floor. He slowly closed the book and waited for us. He motioned for us to come over, pointing to the chairs in front of him.

"He always knows," Tiger said, keeping her voice low. "Just once, I'd like to sneak up on him unawares."

"In this place? Unlikely."

Ezra was dressed in his regular white shirt, a black vest and pants, and finished off with his rune-covered yarmulke, which pulsed a soft violet every few seconds.

I glanced down at the massive tome and read the title: *Ziller's Theorems on the Existentialism of the Personifications of Death.* He tapped a hand on the large book and smiled at us.

It was easy to mistake Ezra for an elderly scholar. His unassuming presence was intentional, designed to convey an image of power at rest, akin to standing at the edge of an ocean at night, the water a murky unknown, tugging at your deepest parts and, simultaneously filling you with dread and excitement.

Once we were about to sit, he motioned for one of the army of servers that were crisscrossing the floor, transporting orders to and fro.

"Come, sit," he said to us. "Just in time for breakfast."

"It's always time to eat in here," Tiger said, sitting down smiling at him. "Hello, Ezra."

"Tiger," he said with a small nod. "You both have news. I see Char has welcomed you into her enclave."

"How do you know these things?" Tiger asked. "Are you omn—?"

Ezra rubbed a finger along his nose.

"I'll answer your question if you answer one of mine."

"Sure," Tiger said. "Ask me."

"Why do you resort to violence as a response?" he asked and pushed his glasses up his nose slightly. "Nine stories could have killed him."

"It could have killed me, too."

He wagged a finger at her.

"We both know that's not true," he said. "Do you have an answer?"

"It's who I am, what I am," she said after a few moments. "I can't pretend to be something else."

"That's the same answer to your question," he said. "At least that's the safest answer I can give you."

"I knew you were going to pull something like this," she said. "Safest? Really?"

"Yes, really, child," he said. "I have no need for subterfuge."

Tiger grumbled, but remained silent.

"Doing some light morning reading, I see?" I asked, pointing at the book. "Do you really learn anything when you read these books? Especially this one?"

He nodded.

"Ziller is quite advanced for his young age," Ezra said. "This is a new edition he wants me to review and correct. I always enjoy discussing these things with him. He has a keen mind. Did you want to discuss the topic?"

I raised a hand in surrender and shook my head without

even attempting to jump into the subject. The threat of a mental breakdown was real if I considered delving into paradoxes with Ezra.

"No, thank you," I said. "I know when I'm out of my depth."

"Do you?" Ezra said with a small smile and glanced over at where Uluru sat. "We shall see."

The server pulled out a small pad and stood at attention next to Ezra.

"What does that mean?" Tiger asked.

"One moment," Ezra said, raising a finger. "Breakfast before battle, isn't that what you always say?"

"That's not what I always say and you know it," she answered. "You're going to have to reveal your secrets to me one day, old man."

"When you're ready, they reveal themselves," he said. "Now"—he looked up at the server—"one full English breakfast and one Peaches special with two egg creams. These two haven't been eating well."

"Peaches special?" Tiger asked, looking at him skeptically. "What's a Peaches special?"

"It's our new signature Pastrami on Rye sandwich with all the works, placed on extra large slices of bread, perfectly smoked pastrami, our homemade mustard, and finished with the sour pickle."

"Isn't Peaches—?" I began.

"Simon's hellhound? Yes," Ezra finished. "We've made this sandwich a little special, just like him. Now tell me what brings you here."

I explained some of the situation with Maledicta and the gem to Ezra. I avoided going into detail since some, if not most, of the clientele in Ezra's place of business could be construed as harboring lethal intent.

"I see," Ezra said when I was done. "How does your partner factor into this equation?"

"My partner?" I asked, thrown off by the question. "What partner?"

"He likes to be deliberately dense," Tiger said, staring at me. "He means, Regina. You know, the love of your life."

I glared at her as a few tables around the deli shifted from casual avoidance to active ignoring at the mention of Regina's name.

"Seems I'm not the only one looking for her," I said, glancing around the floor. Most of them avoided looking in my direction, all except the lone figure in the corner—Uluru. "Why is he here?"

"The same reason as you...breakfast," Ezra said as the plates loaded with food were brought to the table. "That and he probably has a few questions for you regarding a particular thief and her whereabouts."

"I don't know where she is," I said. "Even if I did, I wouldn't divulge it to a Stone Assassin."

"Eat first, talk later," he said. "Tiger, will you be able to finish all of that?"

Tiger looked at her plate which required a small table of its own. The servers had made room next to our table and situated the Peaches special in the center of a table designed to hold the oversized plate. Half of the sandwich was easily the size of an entire pastrami sandwich.

This creation was certainly fit for a hellhound, and I doubted he had any trouble devouring the layers of pastrami. Whether Tiger could match a hellhound's appetite remained to be seen.

"I can't eat all of this," Tiger said, looking down at her plate. "I don't have a hellhound's stomach."

"You take the rest with you to go," Ezra said, getting to his feet. "Now, you two, eat"—he tapped us on the shoulders

—"I'll be right back. In the meantime, I'm sure your guest will be on his best behavior."

"Guest?" I said as Ezra walked away and waved. "What guest?"

"Me," a voice said as I turned back to our table to stare into Uluru's gray eyes. "I requested this meeting."

THIRTEEN

Tiger dove into the sandwich and ignored Uluru as she devoured her food.

I was a little more concerned as to how Uluru could request a meeting when we had only planned our trip to Ezra's this morning. How would he know to meet us here, and why?

"Uluru," I said, keeping my voice composed and motioning to the empty chair opposite me. "A pleasure. Please join us."

Uluru was known as a Stone Assassin. He was the only mage I knew who could approximate Tiger's body-hardening skill with any degree of effectiveness.

Stone Assassins primarily worked as security or body-guards, protecting individuals who had accumulated an extensive and lethal list of enemies. They were some of the best at what they did. It was hard to kill someone who can withstand most physical damage unscathed.

Uluru wore a dark blue blazer over a crisp, gray shirt, and black slacks and shoes. For as long as I'd known of him, he had kept his head shaven, allowing the runes of his dark sect, the Granite Fist, to be viewed easily along the side of his head.

His bronze skin glistened as he accepted the invitation with a curt nod and sat at the table. The symbols along the side of his head gave off a subtle violet glow.

It was both a warning and a source of pride.

Most of the Stone Assassins never made it past the grueling years of training to wear the runes of the dark sect. To exhibit the runic symbols openly meant he had skill.

His exploits had reached even us in the Directive, though I had never had the opportunity to face off against Uluru or any other Stone Assassins for that matter.

I wasn't looking forward to starting now.

"Sebastian," Uluru said, placing two fingers of his hand to the side of his head, briefly covering his runes before turning to Tiger and giving her a nearly imperceptible nod. "Tiger."

It wasn't that the Granite Fist had problems with women —many of the Fists were female. The Granite Fist had a problem with Tiger. They felt she had stolen the stone skin technique from a rogue Granite Fist and tried to pass it off as authentic.

You can imagine how well Tiger accepted that news.

Her initial reaction was...violent.

Tiger paused for a moment to acknowledge his presence before continuing to eat her monstrosity of a sandwich. I paused for a moment, joined by Uluru as we watched her attack her food.

I shook my head after a few seconds and gave him my undivided attention.

"*You* requested this meeting?" I asked. "Why?"

Uluru reclined slightly in his seat, letting his gaze wander lazily around the room before returning his attention to me.

"You're not the slightest bit curious how I knew you would be here to even request the meeting?"

Tiger stopped eating and gently wiped her mouth with a napkin, before washing down her food with some of the incredibly delicious egg cream Ezra had provided.

"We know who you are, the same way you know who we are," Tiger said, placing her napkin just so, on the table. "We keep a low profile, but we're not hiding from *anyone*. That being said, we have a predictable pattern of locations we visit on a regular basis. It all depends on who you are and how urgent your need is—that determines where you find us."

"I see," Uluru said. "You're right. I came here first after being informed you would eventually arrive during the morning."

"Who told you?" Tiger asked. "Your ears in the Granite Fist?"

"Yes," he said reluctantly, the surprise evident on his face. "They assured me you would arrive here either today or tomorrow according to your previous pattern of activity."

"That, and the pastrami here is worth dying for," she said, refocusing on her plate. "Excuse me, I'm famished."

She motioned for me to engage with Uluru, who stared at her with a look of wonder and something else—affront? Tiger cared little for societal norms and made no apologies for it. Her returning to her sandwich was actually her way of keeping things calm.

Also, with the exception of her shoes, nothing else was more important to Tiger than her enjoyment of her current meal. It didn't matter that dawn had been a few minutes ago and she was already eating a meal fit for three.

When presented with food she enjoyed, she made the most of the opportunity. Her history had many nights of going hungry as a child.

She also didn't observe or stick to meal time conventions. Breakfast food was the same as dinner to her—as long as it tasted good and there was plenty of it, she was content.

The other reason she preferred to keep herself occupied with the food was because she knew it irked Uluru on some level. She wasn't above exploiting his rigid mindset to get him upset.

She knew *how* to be diplomatic, but she would rather do away with the pointless posturing, as she called it, and get to the bloodshed right away if it was going to end up there anyway.

No sense in delaying the inevitable.

Her school of diplomacy left much to be desired.

"She is your second?" Uluru asked, glancing at her. "You allow her much latitude for a *mere* second-in-command."

The tone in his voice held thinly veiled disdain.

Anywhere else, those words would have gotten him impaled.

For once, I was unconcerned about the potential destruction because we sat in Ezra's. If there was one place Tiger would refrain from violence, if that could even be believed, it would be here.

She didn't fear Ezra, the same way she didn't fear death, but she did respect him immensely and would go out of her way to keep the peace in his deli.

I think her lack of fear was one of the reasons Ezra gave her so much latitude. I liked to think he looked upon her as one of his unruly and dangerous children.

Tiger glanced up slowly and then looked back at her meal, but didn't continue eating.

She took a deep breath and then let it out slowly before speaking.

"I know the Granite Fist is made up of some of the most fearsome assassins to inhabit dark sects," she said, keeping her voice even and her gaze fixed on his face. "Your reputations precede you."

"You would be wise to heed them, indeed," Uluru said

with a hint of pride. "We are without peer in our stone skin skills."

"I know you know *of* me, but you don't really know me," she said. "Maybe one day, you would be willing to educate me in your stone skin skills. I would consider it an honor to experience them firsthand."

Uluru gave her a small smile and a nod.

It always awed me how people underestimated Tiger, choosing to continue sailing off the cliff of arrogance, rather than taking a moment to assess the very real threat she posed to their lives.

At this moment, Uluru should have realized that her entire posture was one large warning to Uluru. His best course of action would be to decline Tiger's generous—and lethal—invitation and end the conversation as quickly as possible.

"It would be my honor to educate you in our methods," he said. "I understand you have some rudimentary skill in stone skin? I'm afraid it is most likely a diluted and inferior form you have acquired."

I braced myself for impact—the impact of Tiger's fist against Uluru's face, but nothing happened. She nodded and gave him a tight smile in response.

"I know some stone skin techniques, but I doubt it's near anywhere your level," she said, keeping her voice light. "The Granite Fist sect practically created the stone skin technique."

"Not practically," Uluru corrected. "We are the originators of the stone skin. Anyone who claims otherwise is a pretender and speaks false."

It was a bold claim, considering that Tiger's mentor, Adamat, as far as I knew, was one of the originating founders of the Granite Fist sect and more proficient than any mage alive in the stone skin technique.

The information had been obscured by the other founders of the sect over time, and now only a handful of mages knew the truth regarding Mage Adamat and the origins of the Granite Fist.

"Far be it from me to presume to know the history of your sect and its techniques," Tiger said. "Any instruction you will offer will be welcome."

Now I was getting concerned. Tiger had never been this accommodating in regards to the Granite Fist. She didn't detest the sect, but she had little to no tolerance for their overt arrogance and misplaced air of superiority.

She was planning something and hadn't shared with me.

"Then it will be a privilege to share some of the knowledge with one who has a basic understanding," he said before pausing. "I'm afraid I have requested this meeting with an ulterior motive."

"Please share," I said as Tiger returned to her food. "How can we help you?"

"You may have heard of this group"—he casually looked around before continuing—"the Cursed Ones?"

"We know them by another name, but yes," I said as he referred to Maledicta by a more innocuous name. "What are your dealings with them?"

"My apologies, even in a place such as this, or perhaps especially in a place such as this, words possess great power, especially names. I am reluctant to speak plainly."

"Understood," I said with a slight nod. "What do you want with them?

"The Granite Fist was meant to obtain an object of great value from them," he said, measuring his words. "A gem of some significance."

Tiger glanced around, gave me a look and shook her head slowly.

"You don't want to have that conversation here," she said,

her voice flat, "*especially* not in here."

"I was assured there would be no violence while on the premises," Uluru said, giving the room another casual glance. "I was given a pact of safe conduct from Ezra himself while I engaged in my business here."

"No one is insane or suicidal enough to attack you *inside* Ezra's," she said, lowering her voice further. "Ezra doesn't police the streets though. You can find yourself with some unwanted friends when you leave this place. Deadly friends."

"I can handle myself outside of these walls," he said with a degree of superiority. "It is while I am in here that I must be wary."

"You know what I call those? Famous last words," she said. "You want my advice? Have this conversation at the Church or really anywhere else, but here. But I'm just a second,"—she shrugged—"what do I know?"

"Tiger has spoken prudently," I said. "Perhaps we should relocate to the Church where we can continue this conversation without the risk of antagonizing some of the clientele?"

"Are you certain she is your second?" Uluru asked, staring at Tiger. "She is undisciplined, speaks out of turn, and does not know her place. You should allow the Granite Fist to assist you in her training. We understand the principles of discipline among our warriors, especially among the lower ranks."

Tiger nodded and gave me a look.

I nodded before glancing down at my plate of back bacon, sausages, eggs, tomatoes, mushroom, toast, beans, and of course Ezra included one of the most important sides—the black pudding.

I glanced around the floor and saw that Ezra's failsafes were all in place. Nothing would happen in the deli without his knowledge, which meant I could actually enjoy a meal, for once.

I dove into my English Breakfast before it became cold.

Tiger cleared her throat and turned to Uluru.

"Yes," she said. "I agree to your offer."

"My offer?"

"You offered to show me the discipline of the Granite Fist," she said. "I see no better time than the present. Do you?"

"This is not a game," he said, glancing at me, some of the arrogance gone from his tone. "Our discipline is harsh and exacting. The stone skin technique takes years to learn and even longer to master. If I were to instruct you even in the most rudimentary casts, I could show you no quarter. To prevent any misunderstanding, I will refrain from this action. I wish no offense to your leader."

"Oh, I'd say we crossed the road of offense, don't you think?" she said. "You've not only questioned my skill, but you've thrown into question his selection of me as his second-in-command." She leaned forward. "More have suffered for less offense shown here this morning. I accept your offer."

"We cannot possibly unleash violence within—"

"I'm sure Ezra will lend us his back room for my moment of discipline. Unless you feel you're not up to the task?"

"Sebastian?" Uluru asked, looking at me. "Are you certain?"

"If it means I can have a moment's peace to eat my breakfast, then yes, by all means, share the discipline," I said with a nod. "I've always thought she could use some correction. It would be my honor if she were to receive this instruction at the hands of the formidable Granite Fist."

The look of surprise was replaced with one of intent satisfaction on Uluru's face. He was looking forward to correcting my upstart, unruly, second-in-command.

If I was lucky, I'd get through a quarter of my breakfast before Tiger broke him.

FOURTEEN

Ezra, probably sensing the impending tsunami of pain that brewed around us, approached the table.

"Follow me," he said, motioning to us with a finger as he turned and walked away. "Now."

I looked up and then back down at my food.

"My breakfast," I protested. "I just started—"

"It will keep," Ezra said before he vanished into the back.

It was unwise to defy Ezra in the best of times. It was life-shortening to do so while sitting in his deli after being given an instruction.

I looked at my breakfast, took one last deep breath of its delicious aroma and stood, walking away as I followed Ezra to the back.

Once past the double doors that usually led to the kitchen area, I found myself standing next to Tiger and Uluru in a large, empty room. Ezra stood near the doorway and waited for me to enter the room fully before giving us a short nod. Once we were all inside, the door to the seating area disappeared.

"Are you certain you wish to do this?" Ezra asked, looking at Tiger. "You do realize you are still bound by your pact."

"I will uphold my pact," she said. "I don't need to break it to receive instruction from Uluru. Do I?"

"No, you don't, but you may not divulge the origins of what you will demonstrate," Ezra answered. "Can you abide by the rules set in place by your teacher?"

"Don't have much of a choice," she said, looking around. "Anything else?"

Ezra held out a hand.

"Claws," he said. "This is a non-lethal instruction. The Granite Fist would take Uluru's death as a personal insult. And you know my policy on violence while in the deli. Let's not make a delicate situation more volatile than it needs to be."

Tiger extended her hands and placed her claws in Ezra's hands.

"I wasn't planning on using them, you know."

"I know," he said. "I'm just making it safer for you. To avoid any unforeseen accidents."

"You need not concern yourself with my well-being," Uluru said smugly. "I will temper the lesson and only show her a fraction of what she faces. It will be over before she knows it. Only her pride will be bruised."

"In order to provide a robust lesson," Ezra said, glancing at Uluru, "you may want to consider using more than a fraction of your skill. Or it may be over too quickly for her to absorb any information of import."

"I do not wish to injure her," Uluru said, shaking his head. "I will only expose her to some much needed discipline that has been lacking from her training...and life. I will not drag this out longer than it needs to be. It will be long enough for her to understand she is outmatched and outclassed."

Tiger smiled as Uluru crossed to the other side of the room.

"In order to give you as much free rein as possible without creating an incident, all non-lethal or temporarily damaging attacks are allowed," Ezra said, pushing his glasses up the bridge of his nose. "Anything lethal, or permanently disfiguring is prohibited for the purposes of this lesson. Understood?"

"Understood," Tiger said. "Leave him in one piece. Don't break him too badly."

"Understood," Uluru said with a smile. "Minimal damage and maximum discipline." He turned to Tiger and gave her a short bow. "I thank you for the privilege of instructing you this day."

Tiger returned the bow.

"Thank you for the privilege of receiving instruction from you today," she said. "I know this will be an educational moment."

"Very well," Ezra said, moving back from the center. "You may begin when you are ready."

I walked to the center of the floor and stepped close to Tiger. She kept her gaze locked on mine. For the briefest of moments, concern for Uluru flitted across my mind. Tiger was many things; deliberately homicidal when she had no need to be, was not one of them.

She would exert control and explain in the language she was most fluent in, the error of his ways. I would be surprised if this lesson lasted more than three seconds.

"Be nice until it's time to no longer be nice, then be ruthless, unforgiving, and unstoppable."

She nodded and Uluru scoffed while looking at me.

"Be nice?" he said. "This is your advice to her? It is no wonder she lacks discipline. Stone Assassins are not *nice*. We are warriors, and our enemies are crushed against our might without mercy. I. Will. Not. Be. Nice."

I moved away from them both and stood next to Ezra.

Ezra's back room served many purposes.

It was true: violence of any kind was prohibited within the walls of the deli. The only exception was a settling of differences sanctioned by Ezra himself.

It didn't happen often, but it wasn't overly rare, either. There were plenty of individuals who frequented Ezra's with a disagreement to settle; Ezra would allow them to settle their differences in any way they saw fit as long as it remained non-lethal.

Several guests protested at the safety feature, until Ezra explained that if they were that intent on doing away with the formalities of the dispute, he could bypass the strict rules and end their lives where they stood.

Right now.

That usually encouraged compliance.

I looked around and slowly unleashed part of my innersight.

Ezra tutted at me and pulled on my ear to get my attention.

"Are you looking to destroy your mind, child?" he asked, still holding my ear. "What are you doing?"

"I was just examining—"

"Examining? Examining?" he asked. "Your mind can't survive staring into the infinite. Stop that nonsense right now."

He released my ear.

"The infinite?" I asked. "What do you mean?"

"I'll not explain to Char why her new dragon suddenly has matzos for brains," he said, chastising me. "Keep your sight within the room and nowhere else. This is how you got in trouble with that lovely little girl, Regina."

"I was just wondering—"

"Sebastian, I'll do the wondering," he said. "Especially about where we are. You should be concerned with what your second is going to learn in her *lesson*."

"Seriously?"

"As serious as running into me unexpectedly," he said. "Is that something you'd like to do?"

"Not even expectedly."

"Good," he said, pointing down with a finger. "Keep your sight and your focus here."

"Are you sure I can't just—?"

"A small peek," he said with a sigh. "I know you. No longer than a few seconds, or you will find yourself elsewhere and your brain a puddle on the floor."

I had the distinct feeling we were no longer within Ezra's, but since this room possessed no windows and no distinguishing features, I had no way of determining exactly where we were.

Even using some of my innersight, all of the seams of the walls were sealed tight. No energy signatures escaped in any direction.

I nodded and let a small amount of my innersight explore the interior of the room. I didn't dare unleash my truesight. I was daring, but I was not looking to have matzos for brains.

The impression I received was of being everywhere and nowhere at the same time. Ezra's back room was unlike anyone else's back room. It had been rumored that his room was a super nexus of confluence, similar to a singularity of time and space, combining many points in our plane, if not all, into one.

Even if I understood how it worked, there was no way I could explain the glimpse he allowed me. It was akin to seeing every potential outcome of every potential possibility, branching out infinitely before me, in the space of a split-second.

I staggered back and shut down my innersight.

It was too much for me to process, and a migraine from hell squeezed my brain and threatened to crush my skull to a pulp.

Tears streamed down my face as I held the side of my head. The pain was excruciating, converting the dim light in the room into daggers of pain that stabbed my eyes unmercifully.

"I told you," he said. "But you wanted to 'see'. Hold still."

He placed a hand on my head and the pain vanished immediately.

"What did you do?"

"You don't want to know, trust me," he said. "Now focus, the lesson is about to begin."

FIFTEEN

Uluru stepped forward and bowed.

Tiger took a step forward and did the same.

When they both stepped back, and I realized I had never seen Tiger fight another kinetic mage. The Granite Fist mages weren't all kinetic mages, having many disciplines among their ranks, but it seemed to be the prevalent discipline among the most advanced of the sect.

I wondered if the stone skin techniques and the kinetic discipline somehow reinforced each other. I had never had the opportunity to ask Tiger, and she had only been willing to show me if I agreed to an active demonstration.

Which, knowing Tiger, sounded painful.

This *lesson* would allow me the opportunity to see aspects of Tiger's ability without having to evade crushing blows headed in my direction.

They each took a moment to compose themselves and stepped into defensive stances. I examined the energy signatures around them both without looking into the space around us.

The difference in skill between them was immediate.

The foundation of the kinetic mage's ability is the concept of force multiplication and amplification. A kinetic mage takes a small movement, and through their ability and manipulation of energy, they multiply that smaller force through a series of repeated expansions into a force of staggering proportions.

The most powerful kinetic mages have learned to harness the inherent movement of their bodies: their heartbeats, the flow of blood, the contraction and expansion of their muscles, the inhalation and exhalation of air, even the blinking of their eyes—and taken that energy, multiplied it and built that into an avalanche effect of kinetic power, using it as a weapon.

The example of 'a butterfly flapping its wings creating a hurricane on the other side of the world' was fairly accurate, except with a powerful kinetic mage, the butterfly would be several feet in front of you as it unleashed hurricane-force winds with devastating power.

Uluru whirled his arms in two semi-circles in front of his body.

I strained to keep track of the twin blasts of kinetic energy that raced at Tiger. There were no orbs to avoid, and no crackling energy blasts to dodge.

Kinetic energy was invisible.

All I could see was the displacement of energy in the air between them, similar to watching the heat shimmer in a desert.

A kinetic mage apprentice usually knew they had made a fatal error when a blast of kinetic energy punched into them, pulverizing their organs, or a wall of force crushed them where they stood, reducing them to a memory.

The margin for error in this discipline was practically non-existent.

Tiger stepped to the side and avoided the blasts. Some intrinsic part of her ability allowed her to sense or see the kinetic energy before it reached her.

It was possible her body acted as some kind of runic seismograph and could detect the fluctuations of energy headed her way. Even with my ability, it was difficult, if not impossible, to keep track of the attack she had just evaded.

It was what made facing a kinetic mage so deadly, but the focus on this lesson wasn't on her kinetic ability, but rather her body-hardening skill. Uluru was going to demonstrate how his stone skill technique was superior to hers.

This was usually only done in one of two ways. One of the mages would either subject themselves to greater and greater blasts without suffering damage, or crush the other, demonstrating the loser's inability to withstand the pulverizing forces from the attacking mage.

Considering I had seen her withstand, not one, but two explosions designed to obliterate her just last night, before she was thrown out of a nine-story window, I was skeptical he could surpass Tiger's ability.

"You dodge because you know," Uluru mocked. "My stone skin can withstand anything you attack me with."

"I dodge because the best block is not being there," she said. "Unlike the Granite Fist, I don't gauge my power by how much I can withstand before something kills me."

"That is the entire purpose of the stone skin," he countered. "To not test its strength is weakness and fear. It was created as the ultimate defense."

"I just told you the ultimate defense," she said, her voice angry. "The ultimate defense is not—"

"Is not needing a defense?" he mocked. "You truly believe this? Who would fill your head with such foolishness?"

"My teacher," she said simply. "His technique was flawless."

"Was?" Uluru asked. "What happened to your flawless teacher? Did his technique fail him when he needed it most?"

"His technique never failed him."

From what I had been able to discover using Rat and the Directive's resources, Adamat was betrayed ten years earlier by a fellow mage, Bahren, a high-ranking member of the Granite Fist who had sought to eliminate Adamat and take control of the sect.

Their battle resulted in the destruction of the sect head-quarters and the disappearance of Adamat. Bahren survived but was injured and never managed to take complete control of the Granite Fist.

Still, it was his philosophy which dictated the teachings of the sect and why Tiger was viewed as an outcast and inferior practitioner of the stone skin.

The reality was that Adamat was the superior mage, but opted to live in obscurity, only teaching a select group of disciples and swearing them to a life of secrecy regarding the techniques they had learned from him.

Tiger had been one of his most accomplished disciples.

I still had Rat trying to locate where Adamat currently lived—without success. Adamat preferred to remain hidden, and though I inquired, I didn't push too hard.

If she really wanted to find him, I had no doubt she could locate where he was.

"This philosophy of not needing a defense is a good way to die," Uluru said. "This is why your skill is lacking. Your teaching is incomplete and your teacher was wrong."

She flexed her jaw and remained silent, shifting into another defensive stance.

"Very well," Uluru said, sliding into an offensive stance. "I will show you the flaw of this no-defense defense. This will prove to be a painful, but much needed lesson for you."

He moved his arms in a series rapid piston-like motions resembling a boxer shadowboxing. With each thrust of his arm, he would unleash a blast of energy which would appear to travel some distance from his body and then whip around his body, returning to strike him with force.

The blast would hit him and then increase in power.

He was using his stone skin to multiply the force of the blasts against his own skin. It was a creative and dangerous way to increase the force of his blasts.

Without a deep understanding of the stone skin technique, he could easily mis-time one of the blasts—break a limb, cause internal damage, or worse.

Tiger evaded the first blasts, but they were coming faster now as Uluru increased the frequency of the movements. If he kept this up, she wouldn't be able to evade them for much longer.

Eventually, she would need to use her stone skin. The force of his blasts were becoming too strong and moving too fast to avoid easily. He whirled around and unleashed another series of blasts. Tiger had no time to evade.

She would have to take the blasts full on.

I took a step forward and felt Ezra's hand on my shoulder. I glanced in his direction and he shook his head.

"Those blasts—" I said, staring in Tiger's direction. "They're too strong."

"Are they?"

"You disagree?"

"I only disagree with you attempting to prevent those attacks from hitting her," Ezra replied without turning his gaze from Tiger. "Let the lesson play out."

"That's what I'm afraid of."

"She understood the danger when she agreed to this lesson," Ezra said. "Do you think she is in danger?"

"I...no," I said. "At least not any danger I can perceive."

"There may be a danger you cannot perceive, but one she can," he said, still looking at the two facing off against each other. "This will be good for both of them."

"Not if they break themselves in the process."

"Especially if they break each other in the process," he said. "More is learned in failure than in success."

He motioned for me to look at Tiger.

"Observe," he said. "It would appear she is out of options."

I winced as I noticed the energy blasts heading for her.

She closed her eyes and I almost screamed at her in frustration. What was she doing closing her eyes? Uluru was going to smash her to a pulp, and she was closing her eyes?

She kept her eyes closed as she pivoted sideways, allowing the blasts to wash over her without damage. She rotated her body back and squared off against Uluru while thrusting out an arm.

Uluru, who was initially surprised, dismissed her response to this attack.

It was a mistake.

The attack appeared to be an arm strike, but in actuality, she had never stopped moving. When she pivoted, she extended her arm at the exact point when she faced him, but she didn't stop. She kept rotating, and extended her other arm as her body rotated into the pivot.

What looked like two distinct attacks was really one attack with a pause, allowing for an increase in the power of the second strike. It was a kinetic one-two attack that hid the second strike.

Uluru fell for the deception, blocking the first strike by hardening his skin against the initial attack and lowering his defense against what seemed to be a weaker second attack.

The second part of the attack, which was the stronger one, blasted past his defenses and slammed into his chest.

He flew back and landed hard on his back before rolling to his feet, enraged.

"A ripple whip?" he accused. "How? Where did you learn that technique?"

"Probably the same place you learned it," she answered, keeping her voice calm, which only served to make him angrier. "It's quite effective, don't you think?"

"I demand a meeting of the fists," Uluru said, seething as he approached her, "if you dare."

I didn't think Uluru would do anything underhanded—after all, Ezra was capable of stopping him with a thought. I was concerned how far he would let Tiger go in this lesson. So far, she was exerting an amazing amount of control, but this was Tiger. If Uluru pressed the wrong trigger, this situation could spiral out of control and into a lethal confrontation faster than Uluru could react.

"I dare," she said, placing one arm behind her back. "One or two?"

Tiger stepped forward slowly, extending one arm as Uluru did the same. They kept moving closer until their arms crossed at the forearms.

"Weapons pass to receiver," Uluru said, anger transfixing his expression. "Giver sets the paces of the circle."

"One," Tiger said. "How many paces for the battle circle?"

"Five," Uluru said, "if you think you can withstand it."

I flexed my jaw, but remained silent.

A battle circle five paces in diameter, using only one arm to attack or defend against a mage proficient in the stone skin technique usually spelled a broken arm with multiple compound fractures.

Stepping out of the circle signaled defeat.

The mages would have to fight until either both arms

were rendered useless, using one arm at a time, or either one was forced out of the circle.

"One weapon, five paces," Ezra said with a nod as a violet circle formed around them both. "First to step out or surrender loses."

They both nodded.

SIXTEEN

"You should have forfeited while you had the chance," Uluru said, dropping his stance slightly. "No one in my sect class has defeated me during a meeting of the fists."

"There's always a first time."

"I will show you no mercy," he said, as they sized each other up. "You will leave this circle in pieces."

"I look forward to your instruction," she said and deflected his first strike by turning his arm to the side with a small, semi-circular movement, and returned his strike with a forward thrust.

He twisted his body and stepped around the inside of the circle, dropping his hand down and driving forward with an elbow which Tiger allowed to close on her while leaning back and pushing the elbow up.

Uluru rotated around the upward shove, dropping the opposite arm behind his back and shooting the closer arm forward, fingers leading into Tiger's throat.

Tiger smiled at the switch and let his fingers bury themselves in her throat with no effect. This was the true meeting of the fists. Two Granite Fists would face each other in a battle circle and strike each other, trying to exploit the other's weaknesses or cause enough cumulative damage that one of the mages surrendered or suffered a broken arm.

From this moment forward, there would be no more evasions or deflections. The entire strategy would be to force the opposing mage to harden the wrong area of their body with feints and misdirections, forcing damage upon each other until one stepped out or was forced out of the circle.

Still only using one arm, Tiger dropped her arm and struck at Uluru's lower abdomen, changing direction at the last second and driving a fist into his solar plexus.

He read her accurately, hardening his torso as she struck his body harmlessly, her hand bouncing off his body. He side-stepped and swung his arm horizontally, aiming at her head, only to switch direction and arc his arm down on her collar-bone, leading with a hammerfist.

The hammerfist crashed into her collarbone and landed solidly with a deep *thump* as his blow struck. She looked up into his eyes and smiled. For the first time, he looked concerned.

"You should have requested a smaller circle and two weapons," she said, stepping around his next attack and forcing him to miss. "This lesson is coming to an end."

"You speak with false confidence, but you cannot defend adequately with only one weapon," he said. "You have not been trained in our ways and so, you are defenseless against the attack of a Thousand Hands."

He unleashed a barrage of strikes which Tiger managed to deflect initially but quickly lost ground against as he increased the velocity. There was no way she could shift the areas she needed to harden as he moved faster and faster.

Many of his strikes were getting through her defenses, but they didn't seem to be having the desired effect. She main-tained her pace without slowing and started striking back.

When it was apparent he was slowing down, she increased her pace and started hitting him. His breath began to come in short gasps as she disrupted his breathing.

He redoubled his efforts, but it was over, she moved faster and faster until it was all he could do to harden broad areas to avoid being pummeled out of the circle, and still she attacked.

That was when he cheated.

Instead of adhering to the one arm rule of engagement, Uluru used his second arm and launched an attack with both arms as he smiled at her.

She stopped deflecting and began focusing on just hitting him, still with one hand. His strikes seemed ineffective as he hit her repeatedly.

His expression went from one of smug satisfaction to frustrated impotence. She went from using a fist, to using two fingers and hitting vulnerable areas. The first strike to his ribs filled the room with an audible *crack* as she broke a rib.

An audible gasp escaped his lips as sweat formed on his brow.

The next strike was too fast to track as she brought it down on his wrist, breaking several of the small bones. He grunted in pain and put that arm behind him, but launched another attack with the other arm.

"Do you concede?" she asked. "You have demonstrated your skill."

"Concede?" he barked. "You cannot beat me!"

He gestured and released a wave of energy that crashed into Tiger. She bent her knees and forced her energy down, rooting herself in place as she redirected the attack, thrusting her arm upward, palm first.

The energy swirled around her body and shot up as she stood abruptly.

Her palm crashed into the bottom of Uluru's chin and

lifted him off his feet. He rose four feet into the air, hovered at the apex of the arc for half a second, and then came crashing down, already unconscious before he hit the floor.

She caught him before his head slammed into the floor and laid him on his back as the circle disappeared around them. She stepped out and gave Ezra a short bow.

"Thank you, old man," she said, looking at Ezra before turning to the now unconscious Uluru. "For the record, I didn't kill him. I could have, but I didn't."

"You used a Rising Tide," Ezra said with a nod. "You are full of surprises."

Uluru stirred as Tiger stepped close to where I stood.

"You...you used a Rising Tide," Uluru stammered as he regained consciousness. "Not even Bahren managed to use a third degree cast with that level of skill. How? Where did you learn that technique?"

Tiger looked at Ezra, who gave her a small nod.

"Only the names," Ezra said. "No other details."

Tiger nodded and turned to Uluru.

"I didn't learn that technique from Bahren or any of the other Granite Fists," she said. "My techniques come from Silas and Adamat."

"Silas and Adamat?" Uluru said in disbelief. "Impossible. Silas had no students, and Adamat disappeared after the Battle of Rending. Both are thought to have perished."

"I don't know about that," she said, though I had a feeling she wouldn't share even if she knew differently. "I do know Adamat was *my* teacher and he was the strongest of the Fists. Stronger even than Bahren. Only Silas could match his skill."

"There is no record of his having students outside of the Fist," Uluru said pensively as he slowly got to his feet, "but there is no denying your technique. It's too advanced to have been stolen; someone skilled must have shared this knowledge with you."

He bowed deeply to her.

"Thank you for sharing your knowledge with me," he continued and winced as he bowed, holding his side. "Please forgive my arrogance. It would seem it is I who owe you the deepest apology."

"You weren't the only one who learned something today," she said. "I learned my lesson too."

"What did you learn?" Ezra asked her with a small smile. "Please share."

"Violence is an effective answer, but it's not the only answer," she said, surprising me. "Having the power to obliterate someone, doesn't mean I should—at least not always."

"That sounds vaguely familiar, like something I may have said a few times," I said. "In fact I seem to recall—"

"Yes. More times than I care to remember," she said and turned to Uluru. "You mentioned a gem before we had our lesson. Who were you getting this gem from?"

Uluru glanced at Ezra.

"Can I speak freely here?" Uluru asked. "There were some concerns earlier."

"Yes," Ezra said. "This space is secure."

Uluru nodded.

"Initially, I was going to make contact with the Cursed Ones," Uluru said. "But someone else has contacted me instead. This person assures me they can get the sacred amethyst."

"This person...is female?" I asked. "Did you get a name?"

Uluru raised an eyebrow and nodded.

"I was skeptical at first as well—"

"Oh, I'm not skeptical," I said. "If it's the female I think it is, there is a very good chance she is either in possession of the gem, or is in the process of getting it. What is being offered in return for the gem?"

"Twenty million and a sphere of negation," Uluru said, "*if* she can deliver the authentic sacred amethyst."

"Twenty mil and a sphere of negation?" Tiger asked. "Someone really wants that gem." She glanced at me. "I thought the gem was limited use? That seems like a lot of money for something so short term."

"I was of the same opinion," I said, and then I put some of the pieces together, "unless it's no longer a short-term item."

"Meaning?" Tiger asked and turned to Uluru. "The Granite Fist has twenty mil and the sphere?"

"Yes," Uluru said. "The Fist has many assets worth much more than either of those."

"Yet they are willing to exchange these assets for the amethyst? Why?"

"I do not have the details, I am merely facilitating the exchange," Uluru said. "My involvement ends when the gem is delivered and the items are exchanged."

"Do you have a name?" I asked. "For the female who contacted you?"

"She calls herself the Shadow Queen and is certain she can get the gem."

"There's only one female I know who can make that promise," Tiger said. "Did she say when or where she would meet you?"

"That is why you requested this meet?" I said. "You want us to accompany you to the exchange?"

"I am to deliver half the money and the core of the negation sphere in three days," he said. "I do not trust Maledicta or this Shadow Queen, and I am ill-equipped to make this exchange on my own."

"Why not get more of the Granite Fist to accompany you?" I asked. "It makes perfect sense to have bodyguards act as your security."

"I would, but no one except the leadership of the Fist knows about this," he said. "I'm afraid my sharing this information would—"

"You think they're going to kill you," Tiger said. "That's actually a safe bet. Maledicta for sure. They won't want to give up the gem and the Shadow Queen, well, it's safer to assume she will stab you in the back, or the front, and take it from there."

"It still doesn't make sense," I said. "It's too much money for that gem. Then there's the leadership of the Fist keeping this confidential. There are too many variables."

"You do realize they intend to eliminate you once you make the trade?" Tiger said, looking at Uluru. "They can't leave you alive. You're a loose end."

"It has crossed my mind that my time with the Granite Fist has come to a close," Uluru said. "The current leader, Davu, only seeks power. He says it's for the sect, but he was clear about my not sharing this information with anyone."

"Isolate and eliminate," I said. "Makes this Davu's job easier. There's still something off about this."

"You mean besides the twenty mil and a sphere of negation for a gem that's not supposed to be completely functional?" Tiger answered. "Davu must know something we don't."

"The amount and the sphere is a disproportionate payment for an experimental gem, unless..."

"Unless Heka wasn't being entirely forthcoming?" Tiger said. "She is a Wordweaver; I trust them about as far as I can throw them. That and the fact that they left Amina alive. Something always rubbed me wrong about that."

"Three days," I repeated Uluru's words. "We will join you for the initial exchange. Do you have somewhere secure to stay for the next few days?"

He nodded.

"Good," I said. "I think Tiger and I need to have a conversation with some Wordweavers."

"You think they're lying?"

"Lying? No, but a convenient obfuscation of the facts is very likely."

"Uluru, we will meet you here in three days," I said, handing him my card. "Tiger will give you more details and assign some of our people to stay with you, just in case Maledicta gets wind of your location or Davu changes his mind about your involvement."

"Thank you," Uluru said and bowed to Tiger again. "My apologies for the lesson, but you do not truly know someone until—"

"You meet them in battle," Tiger finished. "One of my teacher's favorite sayings."

"Mine too," Uluru said with a wry smile. "He and I got to know each other often on the training floor through many painful meetings."

Tiger nodded.

"We still don't know where Maledicta is headquartered," she said. "Three days isn't much time to find out."

"It should be enough. In the meantime, let's go have a conversation with Heka," I said, as the anger simmered in the back of my mind. "I don't appreciate being maneuvered into a blood debt under false pretenses."

"I don't think she'd go that far," Tiger said, shaking her head. "Now, Aria...I wouldn't put it past her to rope you into something like this against your wishes."

"Us," I said. "If I entered into the blood debt, the Directive is responsible, even if it's indirectly."

"If that is the case, you may need some assistance," Ezra said. "Before you go speak to the Wordweaver, there is someone you should see."

"Who?"

"Someone who can shed more light on the properties of this sacred amethyst," Ezra said. "Someone with a specific knowledge."

"I don't know anyone who can do that," I said. "I barely understood what it did when Heka explained it, and she was giving us the simplified version."

"I know someone else," Ezra said. "Go finish your breakfast. I'll meet you at your table. I trust Uluru can find his way out?"

Uluru nodded.

"I can exit the same way I arrived," he said. "No one will notice my departure. I'm afraid the same cannot be said of you two."

"What do you mean?" Tiger said, giving him a look. "We can do stealthy. Who says we can't do stealthy?"

"Not stealthy enough," Uluru said, pointing at our hands. "You are marked by a dragon. There is no hiding that. I bid you both much luck."

Ezra nodded.

"He's right, you two go back to your table," he said. "I will contact my specialist, and in the meantime you can devise a method of exiting the deli without attracting everyone."

"Slash me sideways," Tiger grumbled under her breath. "You think we can get Char to take this mark back?"

"Even if she could, and I'm not certain she can, I don't think she would," Ezra said. "Char enjoys conflict and friction. Making you her charkin has certainly provided your lives with a heightened degree of danger."

"Which means excitement for Char," I said. "She wouldn't remove the mark if it means depriving her of the chaos and entertainment it will bring."

"You can ask my specialist about that when you meet her," Ezra said, leading Uluru out of the room. "She'll have the information on the sacred amethyst and the mark Char gave you."

"What kind of specialist would have information on this gem *and* a dragon mark?"

"I'm certain, you being the bright lad you are, will be able to answer that question," Ezra said, heading out of the room with Uluru in tow. "Give it some thought."

He left us alone in the room as another door materialized on the far wall.

"What kind of specialist knows about gems and dragon marks?" Tiger asked. "We don't know those kinds of specialists, and if we do, we're usually trying to stop them from sharing pain and death with us."

"We may not know *this* particular specialist but we know of them."

"Who? Who knows about gems and dragon mar—no. He can't be serious."

"It's the only thing that makes sense," I said as we headed for the new door. "He's sending us to go see a dragon."

SEVENTEEN

True to his word, my breakfast was still warm when we got back to our table. I let my gaze roam the room and noticed that several of the guests were making a concerted effort not to notice us.

"How bad is it?" Tiger asked before downing the rest of her egg cream. "What are we looking at?"

"Well, the good news is that my food still tastes excellent," I said, digging into the remains of my English Breakfast. "The beans are still warm, and the toast isn't too soggy. The eggs are just right, and the black pudding is simply delectable. Overall, I would say the kitchen has outdone itself this time."

She stared at me for a good three seconds.

"Well, isn't *that* great," she said. "We can die on a full stomach...wonderful. How bad is it, Gordon Ramsay? As in, how much damage are we looking at once we leave Ezra's, or is the delectability of the food clouding that vision of yours?"

"Not in the least," I said. "I'd prefer not using that aspect of my sight. It would create—"

Ezra came back before I could finish.

"Uluru is safely away," Ezra said. "It would seem you have some new admirers. Perhaps the mark Char imparted to you is more a burden than a gift?"

"You think?" Tiger replied. "I know you have a strict, no-violence policy, but—"

"There will be no violence while you are within the walls of this establishment," he finished, his voice low, but unwavering. "However, my compact only pertains to my domain—the interior of the deli."

"You ever thought of expanding your borders a bit?" Tiger asked, still taking in the interior. "How about a few blocks square of non-violence territory? Like a cemetery. Aren't cemeteries considered sacred ground?"

"You want Ezra to relocate the deli into a cemetery?" I asked. "Not exactly much of an attraction."

"Cemeteries are sacred in as far as that they are spaces where ancestors are buried and respected. In that sense they can be considered sacred," Ezra said, looking around the interior of the deli. "This place is not considered sacred. Rather through a series of agreements and treaties, it is designated the foci of neutrality in this city."

"You're saying this place is the ultimate neutral zone in the city?" Tiger asked. "This place? Really?"

"You expected somewhere else?" Ezra asked with a small smile. "It makes the most sense if you think about. People gather here to eat and enjoy delicious food without overt violence."

"And plenty of covert threats."

"This space transcends all rules established by the Councils or any organized body of authority," Ezra said. "This location is the primal neutral zone."

"So, no erasing any of our new fans while we're still in this place," Tiger answered while gazing at a particularly menacing group of individuals that looked perfectly capable of initiating a lethal conversation. "Because that group over there, looks extra-nasty."

Ezra glanced over in the direction Tiger indicated, and they all looked away. He shook his head and turned back to us.

"No violence can or will occur in this space. Not without an abrogation of the laws of time and space."

"Violence would act as a catalyst to disrupt time and space in this place?" I asked. "It would upend the plane?"

"Yes," Ezra said. "Violence would have a cascade effect, causing me to take a more direct hand in maintaining the neutrality here. Something no one wants, trust me."

"I concur," I answered. "Having you directly involved in any conflict would be the definition of cataclysmic."

"I don't see that happening any time soon," Tiger grumbled, still looking around the deli and giving some of the more daring threats a world class stink eye. "So all bets are off once we leave this place?"

Ezra nodded.

"All bets are off," he said with a mischievous smile, "but... I'll make sure you have a head start. I can't be seen extending you too much favor, but a smidge, well that should be just fine."

"This specialist of yours," Tiger started. "Why are you sending us to see a dragon?"

"Not just a dragon," he corrected with a raised finger. "The only dragon that can give your Enclave leader, Char, a run for her money."

"There's only one dragon dangerous enough to...no," Tiger said with a look of disbelief. "You're sending us to see—?"

"You two are going to go see Black Cynder," Ezra said matter-of-factly. "The only dragon Char respects, even if she would never admit that out loud."

"Did you just say Black Cynder?" Tiger said. "Tell me you didn't say Cynder."

"I did," he said. "You need her help."

"Why would she want to help us?" Tiger asked. "She's a dragon; she's not going to be concerned with our issues."

"She is going to be concerned, and she *will* help you."

"Cynder, the sworn enemy of Char, *that* Cynder is going to help us? Why would she?"

"Because I will ask nicely," Ezra said. "And most people agree when I ask nicely."

"I don't think it has anything to do with you asking nicely," Tiger said. "I think it has everything to do with you doing the asking."

Ezra tapped the side of his nose and smiled at Tiger.

"You may have something there, but I find it always helps to ask nicely," he said. "When I ask nicely, it takes off the edge of inevitability."

"You mean they're going to do what you want no matter what?"

"No, everyone has free will," he said. "They are free to refuse my request when I ask it, and are free to suffer the consequences of their choices. What they are not free to do, is miss our final conversation. I always find that the last conversation—and mind you, everyone has one final conversation with me irrespective of power, great or small—always goes smoother when they have agreed to my past requests."

"Why?" Tiger asked. "What difference does it make?"

"In the larger scheme of things, agreeing to my requests may seem inconsequential," he said. "But many times, those small details can mean the difference between us having a conversation today or ten years from now. Everything is an interconnected skein."

I nodded as I thought back to the situation and realized

that things were much more complicated than I had anticipated.

Heka and Aria were holding something back from us, from me. Regina would surely make a play for a gem worth twenty million. The negation sphere was just an added incentive.

For her, the thrill would be in getting the amethyst from Maledicta just to prove she could. The Granite Fist's motivation was somewhat obscured. Why offer so much for a gem that would become deadly and useless in a month or so? That made no sense.

"The reason for the blood debt is in question," I said. "Heka said any mage that survived the initial assimilation has two months."

Tiger nodded.

"One month before it's irreversible and one month before the mage is corrupted," she said. "I seem to recall the words 'devouring mind and body as the mage in question slowly goes insane' being used."

"After a month, it implodes," I said, recalling the conversation. "What if that's no longer the case?"

"What? What do you mean?"

"If the sacred amethyst is stable—"

"Then Heka hasn't created a time bomb," she said. "She's created a magical weapon capable of creating an Archmage."

"It's possible that was the plan all along," I said. "She said herself they couldn't get the gem back and lost Wordweavers in the attempt."

"If they had a weapon that could create an Archmage..."

"What do you think a gem like that would be worth?"

"A lot more than twenty mil," Tiger said. "That gem would be worth—"

"War," Ezra finished. "If it was truly stable and could shift a mage into Archmage without the detrimental effects of implosion, that gem would convert the shadows of this city into a bloody battlefield, before the conflict spilled into the light. Everyone on the fringes of this city would want it."

"What do you think, Sebastian?" Tiger asked, staring at me. "You know her better than anyone else. What are the odds Regina keeps it for herself?"

Regina never kept the artifacts she 'acquired'. Especially not a gem with the capacity to devour and then implode the target mage. It was too volatile and too uncertain. She wasn't necessarily risk-averse, but for something like that, she would rather sell it and disappear with the twenty million and the negation sphere.

At least I thought so, but people change.

If the gem was stable and she could survive assimilating it into her body...it was easily worth ten, a hundred times that amount.

Would she take that risk? If she became an Archmage Blade-master, she would be nearly unstoppable. I would have to mobilize the entire Directive, and we would still be at a disadvantage. I'd have to call in some hefty favors from unpleasant individuals, favors I would rather not use unless it was a last resort.

The thought of Regina as an Archmage Blademaster transformed into a nightmare scenario in the span of a few seconds. There would be close to no way of stopping her if she became that powerful.

With that much power at stake, there was a real chance she would be tempted to keep the amethyst for herself.

"The odds are not slim enough to discount it as an option."

"Shit," Tiger said, letting her train of thought continue down the rails of my extrapolations. "We'd need the entire Directive to even have a chance at bringing down an Arch-mage Blademaster."

"Even with the entire Directive, it would still be problematic," I said. "I'd have to mobilize The Reserve."

She whirled on me with a look of disbelief on her face.

"The Reserve? What? Fuck no," Tiger said. "May as well drop a runic nuke on the city and call it a day. You can't be seriously considering using those psychos. We can't use them. Did you forget last time?"

"No one has forgotten last time."

The Reserve was a group of beings that swore allegiance to me for saving their leader decades ago. It was an error on my part, I had meant to destroy them after a low-level sorcerer lost his life after improperly summoning a group of them along with their leader. Instead of killing them, I had inadvertently preserved their lives and bound them to me.

Demonology and sorcery are not my strong points.

It was pure happenstance, a cast gone awry, meant to destroy but inverted, and having the opposite effect. To this day, I swore I had followed the grimoire instructions to the letter.

No one really knew what they were, the only things we knew for certain, were: that they took orders from me, orders was perhaps too strong a word, it was probably closer to suggestions, they numbered in the hundreds, were mostly unkillable demons of some sort, and were practically uncontrollable once they got started.

"We cannot use The Reserve," Tiger said. "Not now or ever."

"Then perhaps, Cynder can help you after all," Ezra said, "despite the fact that she is Char's sworn enemy."

"There are occasions where the remedy is worse than the disease," I said. "Cynder could help us or just as easily disintegrate us where we stand."

"I heard disintegration is reserved for those she likes,"

Tiger said, her voice low and dangerous. "If she dislikes you, she tosses you off the Eyrie."

"That would be decidedly higher than nine stories," I said. "I don't think we would survive that fall."

"The Reserve is not an option, that would be a case of the remedy being deadlier than the disease," Tiger said. "If we use them again, everyone will come after the Directive, and I mean *everyone*...friend and foe."

"I'm not quite at that level of desperation," I said. "For now, let's face the risk that is Cynder."

"How bad does it have to be when we would rather face a dragon than activate The Reserve?" Tiger said. "I'm going on the record now and saying this is Regina's fault."

"Only indirectly," I said. "We still don't know how she is involved."

Tiger shook her head and stared at me.

"Don't," she said. "Do not start making excuses for her. Do you need to see the blade sticking out of your chest *again* to realize she stabbed you?"

"To be fair," I said, raising a finger. "The last time she and I fought, she stabbed me first, but...it wasn't entirely her fault."

"Let me see if I understand this," Tiger said, holding up a finger and mimicking my gesture. "Regina is a darkblade mage, one of the most deadliest darkblade mages we know. She buried one of those same blades in your chest...because of reasons you don't fully understand?"

"No, I fully understand the reason—now," I said, feeling uncomfortable going into such detail. It was difficult for me to admit the connection I had created with Regina because of my use of my truesight. The bond created when used fully, linked two people on the deepest level. It was nearly impossible to resist, which was why truesight was never used without the most profound forethought, not like I had done.

"The reason is simple, I used truesight on her without knowing the ramifications of my actions."

"And her reaction when she finally managed to get control of herself was to plunge a blade in your chest?" Tiger said, giving me a look. "Are you listening to yourself? You're excusing her psychotic behavior...again."

"No, she stabbed me because she was still out of control," I corrected. "Her reaction to the truesight bond was...unexpected, to say the least, but understandable, considering the circumstances."

"And now?" she asked. "If you confront her now to try and stop her from getting the gem?"

I looked away.

"Honestly, I don't know," I said. "She didn't have to help me from the void space. She could have left me to Fakul's devices."

"Then *I* would have stabbed *her*," Tiger said. "She knew she didn't have a choice. She had to find you."

"In that you may be correct," Ezra said. "The bond of a truesight is powerful. She may have felt compelled to assist you in locating Sebastian."

"Yet she managed to walk away after locating you... without stabbing you. What a surprise."

"She explained why," I said, recalling the conversation. "She's going for the amethyst and expects me to help her."

"Does the truesight bond turn your brain to oatmeal?" she asked, looking at Ezra before glancing my way. "I'm asking for a friend."

"It cannot implant desire that doesn't exist," Ezra answered. "It only heightens the emotions that are present."

"So we either deal with Regina sooner or we have to deal with her later."

"It would seem that way," Ezra said. "First, go see Cynder.

She may have some useful information for you regarding the gem."

"If she doesn't shred us first."

"Nothing ventured, nothing gained," Ezra said. "Besides Cynder won't take such extreme action, at least not without hearing what you have to say, first."

"That's reassuring," Tiger said. "Don't you have another specialist? One that isn't Char's enemy?"

"Not for this, no," Ezra said with a small headshake. "You'll be fine. Cynder, unlike Char, is level-headed. If she decides to erase you from existence, she will have a rational explanation for her actions."

"Not helping," Tiger answered. "I'd rather not run the risk of getting erased in the first place."

"Ah, you wish for a carefree life?" Ezra said, tapping his chin in thought. "That is an illusion. There's no such thing. Even the most carefree of lives still has its risks and worries."

"I know," she said. "I'm just not in a hurry to shorten it today."

"I can assure you, Cynder will at the very least, have a conversation with you...as a favor to me," Ezra said. "It depends on you, how that conversation ends."

"And Char?" I asked. "How will she react?"

"Char?" Tiger asked. "Who said anything about speaking to Char?"

"Do you really think this meeting is going to go unnoticed?" I asked. "I imagine as soon as we are done, Char will want a word. We are her Charkin after all; she will want to know why we are meeting with her mortal enemy."

"That sounds like a conversation *you* need to have with her," Tiger said. "Leave me out of it."

"If I could, I would, but you bear her mark as well," I answered, pointing to her hand. "You know she will want to see us both."

"Fine, first things first," Tiger said. "We need to leave Ezra's without making new friends." She glanced at Ezra. "Any ideas?"

"I may have a few," he said. "I just need five minutes and your cooperation."

"Five minutes and our cooperation for what?

"To facilitate the distraction you will need to get to your vehicle without being subjected to an immediate attack the moment you step out of the deli."

"If it means leaving here without an entourage, what do we need to do to help?"

EIGHTEEN

"I need you two to draw attention to yourselves," Ezra said. "Something loud and hard to miss."

"Can I smack our fearless leader?" Tiger asked. "I even promise not to harden my hand when I do so."

"That's considerate of you," I said. "I think smacking me would fall under violence?"

"I'll allow it," Ezra said, much to my surprise. "Tiger...no hardening of the skin."

I stared at Ezra in mild shock.

"You'll what?" I asked. "What about upsetting the balance of time and space?"

"This isn't true violence," he said. "You know it's coming, and she will hold back."

Tiger nodded her head with fake solemnity.

"She's striking me," I said, trying to prevent my face from being broken. "That sounds like violence to me."

"The act of striking you will be so unexpected to others, that it will create the diversion you need and give you a window of opportunity to be escorted out of the deli without raising suspicion."

"That will last until we get to the Tank?" Tiger asked. "I'm really not in the mood to fight my way to the Tank."

"Yes. Without it, your enemies will be on you the moment you set one foot off this property," he said. "This way you can get to the security of the Tank and then to Cynder. I highly doubt anyone will follow you to her home."

"Not if they want to see another dawn," Tiger said with a smile as she rubbed her hands together. "This is going to be the high point of my day."

"You don't have to enjoy it so much," I said bracing myself for the smack from oblivion. "You could at least pretend to be reluctant about this."

"I am," she said with mock seriousness. "It truly pains me to think I may have to visit violence upon you."

"Rubbish," I said, waving her words away. "You're enjoying every second of this."

"True, I am," she admitted before turning to Ezra. "How dramatic does this need to be?"

"As dramatic as possible," Ezra said, holding up a finger at Tiger's smile. "Do not break or kill him. I know you know how to pull your punches. I expect you to exert the highest level of control you possess for this."

"I will," she said, serious this time. "And I will sell it. Are the front windows runed?"

"The entire establishment is runed, were you not paying attention when I said this is a primal neutral point of the city?"

"I'm going to need your help then," she said. "I can make it dramatic enough that you can get rid of us and make it look justified. Plus, The Stray Dogs will get some additional street cred for daring to violate not just a neutral zone, but *the* neutral zone."

"Why don't I like the sound of that?" I said. "How dramatic?"

"Depends on the old man," she said. "Can you drop the runes on the table and windows for ten minutes?"

"Of course," Ezra said with a nod. "Done. You have ten minutes to exit in a manner deserving of Death. Do not tarry."

He stood to leave and nodded to the both of us.

Tiger nodded back and cracked her neck as she turned slowly and dramatically in my direction.

"This is going to hurt a bit," she said under her breath. "Just pretend we're sparring."

"Sparring with you has never hurt *just a bit*," I said, matching her tone. "It's usually an exercise in extreme agony."

"If the woman you love can stab you in the chest, and you managed to walk away, this is going to be a cake walk."

"You're never going to let that go, are you?"

"Not while you're still breathing, no," she said with a wicked smile. "You ready?"

"No, but I suppose this is the best and most expeditious way to exit the deli and meet with Cynder without having to engage in a protracted battle," I said. "Seems somewhat ironic that the way to exit without getting into a fight is by getting into a fight."

"Life is funny that way."

"I fail to see the humor in this situation."

"Tick tock," she said. "Focus up and I'll make this look good. The most you'll have to deal with is a few bumps and bruises."

"I'm holding you to your word."

"Would I ever lie to you?"

"Lie? No. Grossly misrepresent the truth? You've done so countless times."

She took a deep breath and let it out slowly.

"Here we go," she said. "Just act naturally."

I nodded as she slammed the table with a fist, cracking the wood.

NINETEEN

"It never fails with you," she said, raising her voice as she shoved the table to one side, then pointed a finger in my face. "Everything revolves around you. You are the center of the universe!"

There was a certain ambient status quo in Ezra's.

You could glare daggers at anyone you wanted, so long as no overt act of violence was expressed. Mortal enemies have managed to sit in the deli, at the same table, and enjoy a lunch next to each other, exchanging subtle barbs and insults, but never, ever coming to blows.

It would be unthinkable to breach Ezra's rules in his deli, not to mention escalate an argument to violence. We currently had everyone's attention, but raised voices were not novel in Ezra's.

Everyone knew better.

People glanced our way but were mostly minding their business, until Tiger punched me in the jaw.

Audible gasps filled Ezra's, followed by several surprised curses from the patrons sitting at the tables around us.

I flew back, crashing into several tables behind me, and

tossing them to the side as the force of the blow knocked me back.

The people in the tables around us, suddenly realizing that they now sat at ground zero, quickly dispersed, leaving the area to Tiger and me.

"Are you insane?" I said. "Have you forgotten where we are?"

"Again," Tiger spat, getting to her feet. "Hiding behind rules and regulations. When it's convenient, you bring up the rules, but all you are is a chickenshit leader who has others do his dirty work. Well, I'm done."

I got to my feet and raised my hands in front of my body.

"What the hell are you talking about?" I said. "I never asked you to do anything you didn't want to do. I'm the one cleaning up after your messes. Who's the one resorting to violence for everything...everything!"

"What did you say?" she said, narrowing her eyes. "What are you accusing me of?"

"Your actions speak much more eloquently than my words ever could," I said, gesturing around us at the destroyed tables. "This is what you do, who you are. You're a walking warzone. Why do you think everyone fears you? Why do you think no one wants to be around you? It's hazardous to their health to spend any amount of time around you."

For a brief moment, she looked genuinely hurt, and I made a mental note not to touch on any buttons that would cause her to really snap—and snap *me* in turn. She was sensitive about these things and the Directive was her only family.

To attack that vulnerability was really taking a risk, but she wanted to sell this and we needed to get out of here without facing an actual battle so I decided to switch tacks and push on another subject that would be slightly less volatile.

"You're calling me dangerous?"

"If danger needed an example of what to avoid, it would look at you," I mocked. "Yes, I'm calling you dangerous. Do you even realize we have to pay beyond a premium just to have insurance coverage? Only because you are in proximity to the Directive offices and vehicles?"

"Don't hold back," she threatened. "Tell me how you *really* feel."

"And your ridiculous obsession with those shoes of yours," I said, pointing down at her feet. "They're overpriced, hideous and gauche. How you even think they are the height of fashion is beyond me. Someone should imprison Louboutin for that unforgivable crime against fashion."

She looked down at her treasured Bifrosts, before glaring at me with death in her gaze.

"My...shoes?" she said. "You're insulting my shoes?"

Murmurs filled the deli as more tables were cleared around us.

"He has a death wish," I heard someone say.

"Someone woke up today and chose this as their last day," someone else said. "I can't believe he went for the shoes."

"At least he didn't attack her looks," someone whispered behind me. "He's not completely suicidal."

"And for the record," I added. "I think you should consider joining the gym. You've let yourself go and I can't have you looking like that *and* being a part of the Directive. We have a reputation to uphold, I'll have you know."

More audible gasps.

She crossed over to where I stood in an instant and grabbed me by the chest, lifting me off the floor with one arm. The look of rage on her face and the threat of pain that radiated from her had me questioning if I had gone too far.

She looked up into my face and smiled.

It was the smile nightmares were made of. My heart constricted in my chest as she took one step back and prepared herself by looking at the large window pane across the floor.

"You can insult me. Insulting my taste in fashion?" she said, her voice cutting through the silence in the deli. "That was low even for you."

"Your taste in fashion?" I scoffed. "If it wasn't for your horrendous taste, you wouldn't have any taste at all."

"Right," she said with nod. "I hope you enjoyed your life up to this point."

She hefted me and began moving toward the large window.

"This is all you know...violence."

"Tiger," a voice cut through the tension of the deli. "What are you doing?"

Ezra.

"Taking out the trash," she said without turning. "Seems you're letting all kinds of scum in this place these days, really lowering the bar in here, old man."

"I don't need your assista—"

Ezra never managed to finish the sentence.

Tiger took two steps forward and threw me. This wasn't a martial arts throw, like one would see in judo or jujutsu, where she would have thrown me over her hip.

This was closer to a javelin throw where a spear is thrown at a target. In this case, I was the spear and the target was the window at the front of the deli.

"What have you done?" I heard Ezra say a split second before I crashed through the window. "This is a neutral zone."

At this point, most of the patrons had been divided into two groups. Those who wanted nothing to do with what Ezra was going to unleash on Tiger and me, and were currently running for the exits, and those who held a morbid fascination with how Tiger and me were going to die for violating

Ezra's rules of neutrality, and stood transfixed in rapt attention as I crashed into and through the large window.

I had initially thought the window was Tiger's target.

I was wrong.

I broke through the window, shattering the pane in an explosion of runically treated glass and kept traveling through space until I saw the real target.

It was the very large and solid matte black chassis of a 1966 Lincoln Continental which was parked just outside of Ezra's. The large and virtually indestructible method of transport I had lovingly dubbed the Tank.

It sat there, exuding an air of violent defiance as I headed straight for it. Daring me to try and damage its surface with my insignificant body.

I could almost hear it laughing.

I slammed into the side of the Tank at speed, bounced off, and crumpled on the sidewalk in a heap of agony. Tiger stepped through the window which was now a fairly large new exit and lifted me up by the throat.

"Put him down," Ezra said. "There will be no violence on the premises."

"In case you hadn't noticed, we aren't on the premises," Tiger said. "Which means I don't have to put him down, until I want to."

She turned slowly and faced Ezra.

Ezra nodded.

"You have no sense of self-preservation," he said. "This is madness."

"No, not madness, I just don't fear Death," she said, opening the passenger door to the Tank. Everyone stood frozen, watching us. She placed me in the Tank and slammed the door closed. "I know you and I will have to reconcile what happened here, but it won't be today. I have things to settle."

"You know you can't run," Ezra said. "There's nowhere for you to run."

Tiger stood still and stared at Ezra before sweeping her gaze across the rest of the customers that made up the morning crowd at Ezra's deli.

"Who's trying to run?" she said. "I know there's no outrunning you. Now, if any of these other geniuses"—she pointed at the crowd in front of her—"feel like coming after me, they're more than welcome to try. Anyone want to make my morning even more interesting? I haven't stabbed anyone in over ten minutes, I'm behind schedule and overdue."

No one moved except Ezra who stepped forward and through the broken window. Once he was outside, he waved a hand and repaired the glass instantly. If I wasn't aching from the recent trip through the window, I would have wondered if it had been shattered at all. I gazed at the front of the deli and I could see the subtle glow of the runic defenses etched in the glass, restored to their full strength.

We were the only ones in front of the deli.

With another wave, I could sense a sphere of silence descend around us, as the glass of the deli became opaque, obscuring the vision of all of the patrons inside.

I lowered the window on the passenger side.

Ezra touched the side of his nose with a finger and pointed at Tiger before nodding.

"Did I sell it, old man?"

"Wait a few weeks before coming back," he said. "If you need to get in touch with me, use alternative means. I'll keep the veil up until you leave. It will appear as if I undid your vehicle. This will only add to your 'street cred', I think."

He shook his head and smiled.

"Thank you," I said. "For this and our meeting with Cynder."

"Ach, this is nothing," he said, throwing a hand up. "Don't

be so quick to thank me yet. Cynder is no easy conversation. She will do as I asked, but it doesn't mean there is no risk. Keep your wits about you. She is as clever as Char and just as deadly. Do not let your guard down and remember all information comes—"

"At a cost," I finished.

"Make sure you consider it deeply before you agree to the payment," he said as Tiger got in the Tank. "Now, get going, I still have to deal with the morning rush."

"Thank you," Tiger said. "I'll see you soon, old man."

"Not too soon," he said and turned to step back into the deli. "I've had enough excitement to last me a few days."

Tiger laughed as we sped off.

TWENTY

Tiger jumped on 2nd Avenue and headed uptown.

The Eyrie was located on the 85th floor of the Empire State Building, which was located at 20 West 34th Street.

It was located on 34th Street and sat just off 5th Avenue, forming the corner of the block at 34th and Fifth. Tiger was taking the most direct route by using 2nd Avenue.

Direct didn't always mean the fastest, especially when dealing with dragons. We would be able to approach and enter the building—it was a tourist attraction after all. Getting to see Cynder would be another challenge to overcome, but we were going to have to tackle this situation one obstacle at a time.

Despite the fact that Ezra requested she see us, Cynder was free to refuse Ezra's request with little to no immediate repercussions from him. It was like he said, he operated on so many convoluted levels of causality, that it was usually in your best interests to agree to his requests.

The life you may be saving, may be your own when you did.

Unlike Char, who moved locations and preferred to be

closer to the ground or even under it—with the Dungeon, Cynder fully believed in the superiority of dragons to such a degree that she felt she deserved to live above the human population, both figuratively and literally.

She remained in one location and hardened the space to the point that it was impregnable. No one had ever attempted to infiltrate Cynder's base of operation, for the same reason no one considered Fort Knox a soft target.

It made no sense and was a waste of time, energy, and resources. You would be better off trying to approach her through more legitimate means.

Ezra sending us to see her was unexpected and surprising. My information regarding her details was scarce because she was intensely private and divulged little to nothing about her personal life.

What little I knew came from Rat's research and it was scant at best. The fact that Cynder was a dragon was known in the shadow world. That information served to instill fear in her enemies.

That and the fact that her enemies had a tendency to take flight from The Eyrie, usually against their volition, cemented her fearsome reputation as a dragon not to cross.

Professionally, she was on par with the status Char held. If Char was the preeminent information broker of the underworld, Cynder was the underworld's ultimate enforcer. From our information, she led a veritable army of security personnel who she contracted out to her clients.

If you were involved in less than reputable business dealings and needed to keep your people safe, you contacted Cynder. She would provide you with the personnel needed to be able to conduct your business in relative safety.

Of course in our world there were no guarantees, and every so often some freelancer who felt they could protect themselves better without Cynder, would suddenly find themselves alone, without protection, in shark-infested waters and holding a bucket of chum.

It never ended well when they questioned the necessity for Cynder's services. More often than not, those who questioned her usefulness became short-lived object lessons in what not to do.

Her personal guard, from my understanding, was made up completely of dragons called the Nine Wyverns or simply The Nine. Whether they were truly dragons or not, was uncertain and obscured in rumor I had no way of corroborating.

What I did know, was that her personal guard were a formidable security detail comprised of nine people who appeared human, and were known throughout the shadow world of our city as a group to avoid, if at all possible.

I would hate to have to go up against one of them—nine would be a suicide mission. No one ever wanted to voluntarily get on Cynder's radar, the same way most people opted to avoid direct contact with Char.

It was unwise to associate with dragons, unless you were one, and even then, dragons were solitary beings preferring solitude to any kind of interaction, dragon or not, and here we were, heading to Cynder's home bearing the mark of her enemy.

In the scheme of things to do that could get you killed, this had to be at the very top of the list.

Tiger continued heading uptown as I took a mental stock of my physical state, making sure she hadn't broken anything in her little demonstration at Ezra's. There were some major aches and pains, but nothing felt out of place. I would be wearing some impressive bruises, along with some minor cuts along my face until I healed myself.

Other than that, I would recover mostly unscathed. I

didn't know if I could say the same about Tiger. I needed to make sure that things between us weren't strained.

Physically, I knew she was fine. I never worried about her tolerance to withstand physical trauma. Her training and techniques allowed her to withstand things that would kill most people.

It was emotionally that she concerned me. As strong as she was physically, her mental and emotional state could be brittle at times. She had come close to a complete meltdown once, in the past.

It was a scenario I didn't want to revisit...ever.

"Throwing me through the window?" I asked as I felt around my cheekbones. "That was your idea of selling it?"

"I had to make it look authentic," Tiger said, her words clipped. "I could have thrown you harder and farther. Maybe I should have."

She was upset.

"About what I said," I started. "You know I didn't mean—"

"Forget it," she said. "You think I'm a walking warzone and you hate my shoes. I got it. Thanks for the update."

"There's no one in the Directive I would want by my side more than you if I had to visit a dangerous dragon or any kind of threat for that matter," I said and meant it. "I know what I said and you know, that I too, was selling it. If I really thought you were a menace to the Directive or the general population, I wouldn't just tell you."

"I know, you'd take action," she said, her voice softening somewhat. "I know you put up with plenty from me and sometimes I can be a handful."

"I do so willingly," I said. "There's no one else I would want by my side as we ride into battle."

"Same," she said. "I'm sorry you had to choose between the Directive and Regina."

That was what was really bothering her.

She was concerned with Regina present in the city that the latter would try to rip me away from the Directive. Regina had tried it in the past.

The truth about the blade in my chest was a direct result of my declining her offer—she disagreed with my putting the Directive before us...violently.

The old saying about hell hath no fury like a woman scorned sounded like firsthand experience. I was certain it was written by a man suffering the wrath of woman he had scorned. Whether or not he survived it for long, I have no idea. What I did know was that the love that burned between two people could be double-edged. It could bring comfort, or it could transform into a hatred that razed everything to the ground.

I had experienced both with Regina.

"There was no choice," I said, my voice hard. "She wanted me to abandon my family, to let you all die and run with her."

"One of the many reasons she and I get along so well," she said. "Like oil and water."

"We may share a bond, but no bond transcends the bond I share with the Directive," I said. "She asked the impossible, knowing I would refuse. It was her escape plan, but I didn't realize it until much later."

"Still, it couldn't have been easy," she said, glancing my way. "I know you don't like talking about this, and I don't mean to pry, but she's back and I have to make sure—"

"I'm not abandoning the Directive for anyone, period," I said. "There's nothing else to discuss. That decision was made and settled long ago. If I ever have any doubts about the choice I made, I have a particular set of scars to jar me back to reality."

She nodded and then smiled.

"So you were saying?"

"That depends, what are we discussing at the moment?"

"My fashion sense is gauche?"

And just like that, we were good.

Tiger was capable of Biblical acts of retribution, but with those she cared for, she was also capable of immense acts of forgiveness.

I didn't know if I would ever truly understand how her mind operated, but what I did know, was that I found myself among the fortunate few she considered her family.

That was good enough for me.

"Absolutely not," I said with a shake of my head. "Perhaps a tad unsophisticated, but certainly not gauche."

"My fashion sense is impeccable and you know it," she said. "That's why Christian agreed to make my shoes."

"I thought it was because you didn't give him a choice in the matter?" I said. "I heard something about you visiting such pain upon him that his future generations would be born in agony as a result."

"Well, there was that, too," she said with her wicked smile. "He knew better than to turn me down. I made him an offer he couldn't refuse."

"And he wisely chose to accept it," I said with a nod. "What's this about the world revolving around me?"

"Actually, in regards to that, I was telling the truth," she said after a pause. "I know you don't believe it, but it's no accident our group is called the Treadwell Supernatural Directive. You are the glue that holds us together. Sometimes, I think you're the only one who could deal with all of us without strangling the group out of frustration."

"There have been moments," I said, looking out of my window as we drove uptown. "But you're wrong. It's named the Treadwell Supernatural Directive because our enemies will always need a target for their ire. I am that target so that you can do what you do best."

"And what do you do best?"

"You don't know?"

"Enlighten me," she said. "I mean, besides being amazingly aerodynamic and crashing through windows with style."

"I did manage an excellent shattering of that window at Ezra's."

"Really?"

"Yes, really," I said, giving the answer some thought. "As for what I do best...I am the bulwark that stands between the world and the Directive. That is what I do best, and if I do say so myself, I am bloody excellent at it."

"Agreed," she said with a nod. "Okay, Mr. Bulwark. whats the plan for getting the information from Cynder and leaving the Eyrie intact?"

"We have to lean heavily on the fact that Ezra sent us," I said. "That's our major leverage."

"Weak," she said, swerving the Tank around mid-morning traffic. "That might get us in the door...might."

"You think she would dismiss a request from Ezra?"

"She's a dragon?" she replied as she nearly redecorated a yellow cab into abstract art, proceeding to smile sweetly at the driver. "Dragons have a habit of dismissing requests from everyone and everything. They have a bit of an ego."

"I'm open to suggestions," I said, turning the problem over in my head. "We're going to be in her home, and she will have her guard there. Not exactly favorable conditions for us."

"It gets worse," she added. "How long do you think we will last after she notices Char's mark?"

"Bloody hell, if I didn't know better, I'd think Ezra was trying to get us eliminated," I said. "But this is typical Ezra."

"True, he doesn't need to try this hard," she answered. "He could just blink and we would be a memory. More likely this is another one of his tests. He must really like you."

"Us," I corrected. "In case you haven't noticed, I'm not going up there alone. I do, however, wish he'd like us less."

"I could always wait in the Tank," she said. "I wouldn't want to get in the way."

I glared at her.

"Fine, don't stare so loudly at me," she continued without glancing in my direction. "I wasn't going to stay in the Tank anyway...you know that."

"His request will get us in the door—of that I'm certain."

"That may prevent us from getting blasted for the first five minutes at least, but I'm going to tell you right now— nine stories versus eighty-five stories is not the same. I would not survive *that* fall."

"Nor would I," I said. "I have no intentions of either of us becoming airborne today."

"Getting into the Eyrie will be difficult, even with Ezra's recommendation," she said. "Getting out is going to be next to impossible."

We arrived at 34th Street and Fifth Avenue.

Tiger drove around the corner and parked on 33rd Street, in front of one of the many awnings that covered the entrances to the building.

This one was located at 1-25 W 33rd Street, and was the only entrance off-limits to tourists and office personnel.

"One impossible task at a time," I said. "Let's go see a dragon."

TWENTY-ONE

The Eyrie had its own method of access apart from the main lobby of the building. This was to avoid the crush of tourists that visited the building daily.

For someone who professed to detest humanity, Cynder had picked a peculiar base of operations. Her home was technically situated on the 85th and 86th floors of the iconic Empire State Building just below the observation deck.

It had several methods of ingress.

There was the heavily guarded stairwell, filled with enough runic traps to convert anyone daring enough to attempt it without authorization to dust by the second step.

We were not taking the stairs.

There were also the two exclusive elevators; that allowed direct access to Cynder's home. Each one was manned by one of the Nine. Trying the elevator by force was an exercise in futility.

If you could somehow get past the Wyvern guard, the defenses in the elevator could be activated remotely. Both cars were extensively runed and could be dropped from any floor, converting the car from elevator to coffin in a matter of seconds.

The last method of entry was reserved for those capable of flight. One corner of the 86th floor was designed as a receiving area for these visitors.

The beings who used this method of visiting Cynder were in a league of their own and had no concern for high winds or precarious placements of landing pads.

Seeing as how neither of us could fly, we would be taking the elevator.

The recessed entrance was made up of a stylized aluminum and black marble awning. Beneath this, and set back thirty feet from the sidewalk sat one, large, black steel door.

In front of the door, stood another of the Nine Wyverns, Alexander. The steel door was an oversized entrance, nearly eight feet tall and half as wide. Alexander blocked most of it, as he stood immobile at the entrance. He wore an impeccable, bespoke, black Kiton wool suit that gave Ox a run for his money in the amount of material used.

A subtly glowing, silver pin of a dragon in flight adorned the left lapel of his suit. All of the Nine wore the same pin. It was a mark of their status as Cynder's personal guard.

His hair, a mix of deep black and slate gray, which matched the neatly trimmed beard covering his face. He had let his hair grow long and had pulled it back in a neat pony-tail. His violet eyes, which shimmered with latent energy—all of the Nine had the same colored eyes—took in the Tank as Tiger pulled up to the entrance.

I stepped out of the Tank and looked up at one of the tallest buildings in the city, marveling at its construction. The last thing I imagined today was paying Cynder a visit.

What was Ezra thinking?

Alexander, imperturbable as ever, gazed down at us as we

exited the vehicle and approached the exclusive entrance. His impassive face shifted almost imperceptibly as a small smile crossed his lips at seeing Tiger.

"Alex," she said as we approached. "We need to see her."

He winced at the shortening of his name.

As far as I knew, only Tiger was allowed to address him this way. It probably had something to do with the fact that Tiger was the only person to face him in battle and still be alive to tell the tale.

"Mr. Treadwell, Tiger," he said with a nod. "Weapons?"

"Always," Tiger said, demonstrating her claws. "He just has his usual blades, but upgraded."

"Impressive claws," Alexander said as he admired them. "May I examine your blades, sir?"

"Of course," I said, producing my twin karambits. "How have you been, Alexander?"

"Adequate, sir," he said. "Also a substantial upgrade on your weapons. Goat does good work."

"Thank you, I'll make sure to pass on the word."

"Please do," he said before moving onto the purpose of our visit. "She is expecting you. Please observe the etiquette of House Cynder. May you have a productive visit."

"Will do," Tiger said as Alexander returned my blades. "Who's on the elevator?"

"Bea," Alexander said after a pause. "Do you require I escort you personally?"

"No," Tiger said as a scowl flashed across her face. "We'll be fine. Your boss likes to do things like this. I promise not to try and rip Bea's throat out."

"Emphasis on *try*," he said, shaking his head. "Out of all the Nine, why did you choose her as your nemesis?"

"*I* didn't choose *her*," Tiger replied, staring into his face. "She chose *me*."

"You had an opportunity to decline the invitation, you refused."

"I wasn't going to let her think I was weak," she said, tapping him on the shoulder. "You know me better than that."

"I do," he said. "Watch your step in there. Lady Cynder has been dealing with some difficult clients as of late. She's not in the best of moods."

"Wonderful," Tiger said, moving past him. "Thanks for the heads up. Whenever you have a day off, I'd really like to test these claws out."

Alexander nodded and another small smile crept across his lips.

"I'll check my schedule and let you know."

"You do that," she said as she headed down the corridor which led to the elevator. "Call me."

I approached Alexander and let Tiger get halfway down the corridor before I spoke. The distance didn't matter; Tiger had uncanny hearing—which I always felt was a byproduct of her kinetic ability.

"Lady Cynder does know Ezra sent us?" I asked as I looked up into his face. "I would hate to intrude upon her time. Especially if she is dealing with difficult clients." I glanced down the corridor at Tiger. "I'd rather not have to deal with an incident."

"As long as Tiger doesn't antagonize Bea on the way up, you should make it to the Eyrie intact. If she does, you won't."

"I know no one approaches the Eyrie unannounced," I said. "Just like I'm certain Bea on the elevator is no coincidence."

"I don't pretend to know the workings of Lady Cynder's mind, sir," he said, his deep voice filling the corridor. "Rest assured, she knows you're here and has allowed you access.

The last guest who arrived this morning left from the Eyrie. They did not possess the power of flight."

"That's not very comforting."

"I trust you will be using the elevator. Please head upstairs."

I nodded and kept moving forward.

It was another thirty feet down a rune-inscribed corridor before we reached the elevator doors. Alexander had only requested to see the weapons and not disarm us, because realistically, unless Tiger or myself carried some kind of runic thermonuclear device, any weapon that we brought upstairs posed little to no threat.

I do believed that when he viewed the weapons, that information was transmitted among all of the Nine. Somehow—most likely through some working of Cynder's—they were mentally linked and had the capacity to exhibit activity similar to a hive mind.

It was part of what made them so fearsome as a security force. Imagine facing a group of highly skilled and trained individuals that could operate seamlessly as one unit.

That was without the variable of them not being human; throw in the supernatural component, and it was pointless to try and take them down.

A few had tried—factions looking to make a name for themselves by defeating Cynder's security. They had only gained recognition as victims. There were some prominent security companies who thought they could oust Cynder from her position as the premier security firm in the city.

They were mistaken.

The directors of those firms either quickly saw the errors of their ways, or never saw anything ever again, retiring mysteriously, suddenly, and permanently.

Cynder exhibited no tolerance for challenges to her

authority. Char's mark weighed heavily on my hand as we waited for the elevator to see Cynder.

"You realize she could take our visiting her with this mark as the height of insult?" Tiger asked. "She could cut us down before you get to say a word."

"The thought has crossed my mind once or thrice," I said. "But thank you for the reminder."

"Just making sure you stay in the present," she said. "If we're going to die, I want to see it coming."

"Oh, I'm certain Cynder will make sure we will see it coming," I answered. "Somehow, something like this gives me the impression she would take matters into her hands personally."

"Good," Tiger said. "That's the way it should be."

The elevator door whispered open and we stepped in.

TWENTY-TWO

Inside the elevator stood a heavyset woman with caramel skin and shoulder length straight black hair which framed her face. Her body was a cross between a powerlifter and a gymnast. Standing nearly six feet tall, she wore a bespoke black Tom Ford skirt suit that fit her perfectly.

Her glowing silver pin of a fearsome dragon in flight adorned the left lapel of her suit. Sheathed to one thigh, rested a short, silver sword designed to make quick work of any enemy foolish enough to stand before her in battle.

Like Tiger, she wore Louboutins, but unlike Tiger, these were Mado Lace up Leather Over the Knee Boots with heels that added several inches to her height and doubled as deadly weapons.

Although there was no hierarchy in the Nine—at least not to my knowledge—this woman, was one of the most fearsome of the group.

Her violet eyes took us in as we entered the elevator. The door closed silently behind us and the elevator ascended.

"Beatrix, a pleasure as always," I said. "Lady Cynder is expecting us."

"She is," Beatrix said with a slight nod. "The pleasure is mine."

"Beatrix," Tiger said with a curt nod, "you look good."

"Tiger," Beatrix replied with a nod of her own, "it has been some time. It's good to see you...alive."

Tiger smiled.

"Lady Cynder has you on elevator duty?" Tiger said, looking around the interior of the lavish elevator car. "Who did you crush without permission?"

"No one—yet," Beatrix replied. "But the day is still young. I never know what clueless moron will grace my elevator with delusions of grandeur requiring me to bring the harsh boot of reality down on their unsuspecting head."

"Are you sure you can even fight in those things?" Tiger asked glancing down at Beatrix's boots. "They look uncomfortable if you have to stand in them for any length of time."

"You'd be surprised at what you can adapt to given the proper stimulus," she said. "I see you have upgraded your weapons. Have they been tested against a worthy adversary?"

"Not yet. The funny thing is, I haven't encountered a worthy adversary—yet," Tiger replied. "Maybe you could point me in the right direction."

"She can't," I said immediately. "Beatrix is busy handling the elevator. She doesn't have time to point you anywhere except off the elevator when we get to the Eyrie."

"Sebastian," Beatrix answered with a dangerous smile, "you would't deprive me of the opportunity to converse with your second-in-command, would you?"

"If by converse, you mean wreck this elevator and partial sections of the building, then yes, I would deprive you."

"Another time then," she said, "second-in-command."

"Another time," I said. "Preferably never."

"I look forward to having a prolonged conversation with you, Bea," Tiger said, risking our lives by using the nickname, "perhaps when Cynder trusts you with more responsibility than ensuring an elevator reaches its destination safely."

Beatrix laughed.

"That's why I like you Tiger," she said. "You have no sense of self-preservation. Very few would have risked their lives with that response."

"That's me," Tiger replied. "Living on the edge."

"You have no idea," Beatrix replied as we reached the top floor. "I truly hope one of you can explain those marks. If not, I'm afraid this may be the last time we speak, and that would be a shame."

We arrived at the Eyrie.

The elevator doors opened and Beatrix pointed us forward with a nod.

"This I believe is your stop," she continued. "Good luck, you will need it."

We stepped out onto the floor proper.

The space was an art deco minimalist's dream home. Plenty of space with sparse furniture situated in strategic locations around the floor.

The floor plan resembled a renovated loft. Open living areas fit seamlessly together and bathed in plenty of natural light. All around us, every wall was comprised of windows, allowing for one of the most unobstructed views of the city in every direction.

Just outside the elevator doors stood another of the Nine. This member was unfamiliar to me. His energy signature equaled Alexander, but was considerably less than Beatrix.

Even though I noticed the member of the Nine, my attention was immediately riveted by the overpowering presence in the center of the room sitting behind a desk directly opposite the elevator doors.

"Francis, please prepare the landing pad," Cynder said without looking up from some papers she was reviewing. "We have some guests arriving in a few hours who would prefer discretion."

"Yes, Lady," Francis said, giving us a circumspect glance before leaving the main area with a nod. "As you wish." He vanished through a side door which I noticed hid a stairwell leading up to what I assumed was the landing area.

Cynder placed the papers she was holding down on the desk in front of her and gazed upon us. It was, in all actuality, the first time I had stood before her and the realization hit me like a blow.

The resemblance was uncanny.

She and Char were related somehow.

Bloody hell.

"You see it," she said, focusing on me, her voice a husky imitation of Char's elderly speech. "Does your second share your insight?"

"Slash me sideways," Tiger said as she stared at Cynder. "You've got to be kidding me."

"I'm going to take that as a yes," Cynder said with a disarming smile. "How is my dear older sister doing these days?"

"Older sister?" I asked still dumbfounded, which explained my phenomenal eloquence. "I didn't realize you two were related."

"Very few people have dealings with both of us, much less personal access to us both," she answered. "You happen to be either very favored or very unlucky. We'll find out which before this visit is over."

I took a moment to collect myself and managed to get my breathing under control. In those moments, I allowed my vision to go wide, taking in not only Cynder's home, but Cynder herself.

Once the family resemblance was apparent it was difficult to unsee. Cynder appeared to be a much younger Char, though I knew they had the ability to manipulate their outer appearance, this human form seemed to be their preferred state.

She wore a darker gray robe than Char, which was simple in its design, but bore the same repeating white dragon in flight motif. I had to assume it was some sort of family or House crest.

I should have recognized it, seeing as it was an exact image of the pin the Nine wore on their suits. For someone who could see more than most, I did have the occasional glaring blind spot.

Her long black hair cascaded down her back in an intricate braid, contrasting against her pale skin. She was nearly the same complexion as Char, but her skin didn't glow to the same extent as Char's.

The energy signature she possessed was overwhelming and I could tell she was actively suppressing it from us.

"Ezra sent us," I said, my eloquence knowing no limits. "He said you could help us."

"You are Charkin," she said, leaning back and tapping her chin with a finger as she continued gazing at us. "What was my sister thinking? You're not even wyvern."

"No, we are—"

"Sebastian, I know who and what you are," she finished. "Char may fashion herself the information broker of this city, but she's not the only one who knows what happens in the shadows."

"I was informed that you and Char were mortal enemies, everyone believes you are mortal enemies," I said. "Even Ezra led me to believe this to be true."

"Everyone except Ezra knows the truth we want them to know," she said. "Ezra knows the truth, but his deli has too many ears and he likes to keep himself entertained, thus he propagates the fallacy."

"He lied?" Tiger said. "Deliberately?"

"Ezra is Death," she said. "There is no being closer to the truth than he. Death is honest, sometimes brutally so, and on occasion must bend the truth to prevent a greater pain from being created."

"I can't believe he lied to us," Tiger said. "Why not tell us the truth?"

"You weren't paying attention," Cynder said. "If you were informed that we were mortal enemies, then technically that is correct. However, we are not in the strictest sense mortal. Which means that the truth is—"

"You are much more than mortal enemies," I finished. "You have a deeper bond that transcends mortality."

"We are dragons," she said. "Your entire lifetimes are like the passing of a summer's day to us. My kind barely acknowledge your existence—with the exception of a select few of us, like my sister and me. To Ezra, we are all fleeting thoughts in the consciousness of time—even dragons."

"That is incomprehensible," I said.

"Don't bother trying to wrap your limited minds around the concept of Ezra and Time," she warned. "That train of thought will only give you a headache or short-circuit your delicate brains."

"Why did he send us here, then?" Tiger asked. "He had to know how you would react."

"Explain the marks my sister gave you," she said by way of response. "Lie to me, and I kill you where you stand."

Tiger glanced at me and I cleared my throat, suddenly feeling parched.

"I sought to deceive her," I said, "by creating a false artifact."

"Daring but foolish," Cynder said with a nod. "Did you really think you could?"

"I did," I said. "At least until we met her again."

"Why did you do it?"

"The artifact was too dangerous to be left in the world, even with your sister," I said. "I took a calculated risk."

"Not just you, but your entire Directive."

"Yes."

"You felt The Gauntlet of Mahkah was too dangerous for *my* sister? She must have gotten a tickle from that."

"I didn't get a sense of levity from her at that moment."

"Oh, trust me, if she had been angry, we wouldn't be having this conversation," she said. "As amazing as this may seem, she likes you...evidently enough to make you part of our family. Continue."

"I admitted my deception and claimed all responsibility for its implementation," I said. "Understanding that the consequences were also solely mine to bear."

Cynder nodded.

"Spoken like a dragon," she said. "We'll come back to that. Go on."

"When she was about impart her judgment, Tiger spoke up"—I glanced at her—"she didn't let me take the blame alone. She wanted to share in the consequences as well."

"Without knowing what they were going to be?"

"Yes, did it matter?" Tiger said. "The Directive is my only family."

"Some would have thought it prudent to at least inquire what the consequences were going to be," Cynder said. "But I do understand your motivation."

"It was a test," I said. "She wanted to...well I don't know exactly the details of what she wanted to test. To be honest, I'd never encountered this situation before. I have a close friend looking into dragon marks, but even he is finding it difficult."

"Because dragons like my sister rarely create kin," Cynder said. "And now she has created two of you."

"You knew," I said as the realization dawned on me. "You knew the moment we were marked."

She raised a hand in response and I saw the image of a white dragon in mid-flight on the back of her hand.

"Of course I knew. We are connected through this, through my sister," she said. Yet you still do not know what it means to be Charkin. I'm afraid that will be a difficult and painful lesson for you both, but that is not why you are here. Why are you here?"

"Ezra sent—"

"Wrong," she said, cutting me off. "You are not here because of Ezra. Do not insult my intelligence and think before you speak, little brother, or I will be forced to cull the family tree. Try again."

If my mouth had been parched before, it had gone positively Saharan in the next moment. I could not forget that while Cynder looked human, she was far from it. I was sure there would be some repercussion from Char for her killing me, but it wouldn't matter. Char was her sister. They would smooth it over somehow and I would still be dead.

I gave my next words profound thought.

TWENTY-THREE

"I'm here to partake in a rare and singular opportunity."

She raised an eyebrow, but remained leaning back in her chair.

"Do tell," she said. "What is this singular opportunity?"

"Confronting Regina and resolving our past."

"Why would you want to do that?" Cynder asked, looking to the side. "Let her have the jewel and the money. What does it matter to you? You have a Directive to run. Leave the past in the past."

My intuition told me my next answer was pivotal.

"Somehow—I don't know how—the sacred amethyst is stable," I said, knowing in my bones I was right. "If we don't act, we will unleash a weapon of devastating power on the world. I can't let Regina have that gem."

Cynder remained silent, but stared at me...hard.

"It is stable, to a point," she said. "If she assimilates that gem, she will have access to untold power. Power you cannot let her have. Why are you here, Sebastian?"

I knew she didn't mean my actual location. That would be a foolish question. She was going deeper. What was the purpose of going after the sacred amethyst, of making the blood debt with Heka? What was it all for?

"Because I unleashed my truesight on Regina and created this bond between us," I said. "Because I have yet to face the consequences of that action—and I must. If I don't, she will get the sacred amethyst and use it to increase her power."

"What would she do with the power of an Archmage?" Cynder asked. "What do you think she will do?"

I was speechless, because the first thought that came to mind was impossible for me to conceive. There was no way Regina would go that far.

Tiger gave voice to my worst nightmare.

"The first thing she's going to do is remove the obstacle to what she wants more than anything else," Tiger said. "That would be her first move."

"No, she wouldn't," I said. "She's twisted, but she's not evil."

"Sebastian, you're right," Cynder said. "She's not evil, she driven, and she has been spurned. You rendered her powerless and she aims to correct that. How do you think she will go about it?"

I glanced over at Tiger who nodded at me with her jaw set.

"She will remove the obstacle to what she wants most," I said. "If she gets the power of the sacred amethyst, her first step will be to destroy the Directive."

Cynder nodded.

"Now, knowing that, why are you here?" Cynder asked. "Why did Ezra send you here?"

"To confront this truth, but more importantly, you know how to destroy the sacred amethyst."

"I do," Cynder said. "The cost though...the cost will be the steepest one yet in your life. Are you sure you want to proceed?"

"Do I have a choice?"

"A valid question," Cynder said. "In all honesty, a question worthy of a dragon. The answer is, no. If this concerned only you, perhaps, but you are Charkin now. You have a Directive to protect and you have a group of darkmage assassins to prevent from spiraling out of control. I'm afraid you do not have a choice in this matter."

"Did I ever?"

"Yes," she said and her voice sounded sad for a brief moment. "The day you unleashed that truesight on your love, you set all this in motion. That was the day, the moment, you had a choice. Now you must face a new choice, one you will not want to make, but one you must."

"I understand," I said. "I'm ready."

Cynder shook her head slowly.

"You only think you are," she said. "I will show you how truly unprepared both of you are. You have three days. We will make the most of what little time you have."

Cynder pressed a button on her desk.

"How did you know we had three days?" Tiger asked as Beatrix appeared in front of the elevator. "We just found out that information this morning with—"

"Uluru," she finished. "Yes, I know."

"Lady Cynder?" Beatrix asked. "How long?"

"They only have three days. I only hope it will be enough," Cynder said, staring at us. "Take them home. After today, we won't be meeting again until they're done...or dead.

"As you wish," Beatrix said and bowed. "Follow me, please."

She turned and stepped back into the elevator.

TWENTY-FOUR

We followed Beatrix into the elevator.

The doors closed behind us, obscuring Cynder from sight. Beatrix turned to us once the doors had closed.

"My first question: what is it that you think Cynder does?"

"It is my understanding that she provides security personnel to influential individuals," I said. "Individuals from all strata of society. Some of them reputable, most not."

"That is only partially correct," Beatrix replied. "She does much more."

"She's a check and balance, like Char is in the information world," Tiger said. "She's the reason there aren't more groups like Maledicta on the streets."

"Yes," Beatrix said with a small nod. "Insightful. Cynder is what is called a necessary evil. She maintains a precise balance."

"A balance that is being threatened," I said. "Because of the sacred amethyst?"

"Because of Regina *and* the sacred amethyst , which means this comes back to—"

"Me," I finished. "The balance is in danger because of me."

"You answered her correctly," Beatrix said as the interior of the elevator began to glow a soft orange. "That was impressive. By all accounts, she is more exacting than Char. The fact that you passed her test says much about your potential, and reinforces Char's decision to make you Charkin."

"Her test?" I asked. "What part was the test?"

"You were informed that Char and Cynder are mortal enemies," she said. "The most prudent course of action would have been to desist and find an alternative method of locating the gem. Yet, you continued undeterred."

"Ezra lied," Tiger said. "That was unfair."

"Did he, though?"

"I don't think he was being completely honest with us."

"I'm certain you can take that up with him when you see each other again," Beatrix replied as she began touching panels on the interior of the elevator. "Why did you agree to fight your way out of Ezra's?"

"What do you mean?" I asked. "It was the best way to leave the restaurant without having to fight our way to the Tank."

Beatrix paused in her pressing of panels and stared at us both for a few seconds, before shaking her head.

"You're both truly like children," she said. "Do you really believe it was beyond Ezra's ability to prevent some patrons from following or attacking you to your car?"

"You mean I was assaulted for nothing?"

I glanced at Tiger who smiled back at me and shrugged.

"No, not nothing," Beatrix said. "You must be willing to see beyond what you see."

"It's beginning to dawn on me," I said. "It was a test of our commitment to each other and the Directive."

Beatrix nodded.

"Yes, through every step of this day you were being test-ed," she said and pressed another series of panels. "Do you know why?"

"Cynder alluded to it," I said. "The cost."

"You are finally paying attention," she answered. "Now we go home to get you ready. You don't have much time."

"Three days is no time at all," Tiger said, frustration creeping into her voice. "What are we supposed to do with three days, besides get weapons?"

"Nothing, on this plane, but we are going home," Beatrix said. "Much can be done with three days...there. There, you will not get weapons. There you will hone the weapons you must become."

"Why is Char doing this?" I asked. "I have to assume this is Char's doing since she is the older sister. Why?"

"She told you," Beatrix said. "When you accepted her mark, what did she call you?"

I drew a blank, but Tiger remembered.

"She called us her weapons, to be used at her discretion."

"That is why," Beatrix said. "This situation with Maledicta is greater than you can imagine. What do you do with weapons before a protracted battle?"

"You hone them," I said. "You make sure they are ready to be used."

"Consider yourselves in the process of being honed."

"Just us two?" Tiger asked. "Against all of Maledicta and Regina?"

"Ask me that question again in three days," Beatrix said. "I look forward to hearing your response."

She pressed another button and the elevator shunted side-ways as the interior runes exploded with violet energy.

"If it's not on this plane," I asked, "where exactly is home?"

"You are finally starting to ask the right questions,"

Beatrix said with a small smile. "You are traveling to a place rarely visited by non-dragons. You are going to the home of the Charkin."

"Who's going to do this honing?" Tiger asked warily. "Is this your department? Are you the resident honer?"

"You ascribe too much responsibility to my position," Beatrix said. "If I were given this task, I would in all likelihood, kill you both."

"I vote you remain on elevator duty then," Tiger said immediately. "No offense."

"None taken, we are wiser when we know our strengths and limitations," Beatrix said. "No, this task belongs to the only one qualified to execute it in such a short time."

"There's a training dragon waiting for us at this home?" Tiger asked. "Someone qualified?"

"You could say that," Beatrix replied. "Someone imminently equipped to get you where you need to be."

"Why does this sound painful?"

Beatrix smiled.

"It will be a necessary pain."

"Usually when someone says a pain is necessary, I've discovered that they aren't the ones experiencing the pain."

"Every one of the Nine have experienced this pain," Beatrix said. "You will not be brought to our level—not being dragons—but you experience an ascension of sorts."

"Ascensions always hurt," Tiger said.

"Metamorphosis is never a painless process," Beatrix said as the elevator came to a gradual stop. "We are here. My advice to you is this: listen and exceed whatever your preconceived limits are. You are stronger than you imagine."

"Thank you," I said.

"Don't thank me yet," she said as the doors opened. "There will be moments when you'll curse me and all dragonkind. Do not let your emotion take control." She gave

Tiger a pointed look. "Maintain your control at all times. Three days will feel like three years at times. Trust the process, even when you don't understand it."

"Oh, this is going to truly suck, isn't it?" Tiger said as we looked past the doors into a large, open room equipped with weapons and etched runic circles on the floor.

Beatrix nodded.

"She's waiting for you," Beatrix said, extending an arm out into the room. "Surprise me and make it through this."

In the center of the floor, wearing a simple white robe with a dragon in flight motif, stood an elderly woman who turned from the windows and narrowed her eyes when we stepped off the elevator.

Char.

TWENTY-FIVE

I took in the space as we stepped off the elevator.

It was as if we had stepped into the sitting room of a large mansion. Everything was made of white marble—floors, walls, and even the ceiling.

The large windows that were evenly spaced along the walls—ten in total, five on either side—revealed an expansive countryside of the deepest green I have ever encountered. Off in the distance, past the large field, I could see an enormous, dark forest.

To the side of the forest, I saw a large body of water. Whether it was a lake or some portion of an ocean, I had no way of telling. The sky itself was a wonderful hue of pink and red, mimicking a perfect sunset on our plane.

A peaceful silence permeated the room and the land beyond.

Char faced us with a piercing gaze. She smiled slightly when she saw Tiger.

"Bas, Tiger," she said as the elevator disappeared behind us. "Welcome to my home. I take it Cynder has approved of you."

"I had a feeling you were behind all of this," I said. "Why not do this in the Dungeon?"

"You always were astute, why don't you tell me?" Char said, looking around the floor. "Tell me what you see."

The space we stood in wasn't a sitting room. It had a very specific purpose. I paused a moment to take in the immense room. It was furnished as an immense magical training hall. The circles on the floor were designed according to specific disciplines.

It was similar to the lower level of the Dungeon minus the conference area. This was a room dedicated to learning mystical arts and doing battle with them.

Half of the floor was thick matting designed to facilitate fighting. The runes which covered the surfaces were both familiar and alien. Just when I thought I could decipher what I was looking at, the symbol would shift and transform into something completely unfamiliar.

I discovered most of the runes were beyond me; the very few I could decipher touched on the abilities Tiger and I possessed, but it went much deeper than that. When I looked down, I noticed that the circles were designed as training circles. I had never seen circles like these in any of the sects I had trained in.

"I know these are training circles," I said. "Though, I've never seen these particular type of circles."

"You wouldn't have, not unless you were a dragon," Char said with a slight nod. She pointed over to a table on the far side of the room. On the table was a large pitcher with a clear liquid. Next to the pitcher sat two empty glasses. "Before we begin, I need to prepare your bodies and minds. Take one glass each and drink an entire glass. Only one, mind you."

"What is it?" Tiger said as we walked over to the table. "Dragon juice?"

"It will allow you to withstand the rigors of what comes

next," Char said. "Drink. Your preparation starts the moment you do."

"We only have three days," Tiger said, glancing Char's way. "I don't know how much you think we can learn—"

"Time isn't linear here," Char said. "Think of time as a fluid concept while you're in my home. Go, drink."

"Will we be able to see more of your home?" I asked, curious as to the size of the property. "This architecture is fascinating."

"Thank you," Char said. "It took many centuries to complete. Sadly, this is the extent of my home that you will experience on this visit. Perhaps, if you come back, I will show you the library. This time, however, we must be singular of thought and action."

Char motioned for us to drink.

We each filled one glass with the clear liquid. Tiger brought the glass up to her face and examined it. She gave me a look and then stared at Char.

"What does this do?"

"You think of time as a river, flowing in one direction only," Char said, moving an arm in one direction. "Once you drink that, while you are in my home, time becomes an ocean, allowing you entry at various points and giving you the limited ability to travel forward and back within it."

"Can we take this back with us to our plane?" Tiger asked. "This would be perfect when facing enemies."

"Only if you want to destroy the plane," Char said. "Bas, you wanted to know why we could not do this in the Dungeon—that's why. If I managed to alter the flow of time, it would undo fundamental aspects of the plane. Only Ezra and primal forces like him have that degree of control there. I, for all my power, do not."

"But here in your home," I said, still looking around. "On this plane, you can?"

"Yes, on this plane, your three days can be as long as I need to help you learn what you need to learn," she answered with a nod. "Now drink and let's begin."

Tiger and I each drank one glass of the clear liquid. It tasted like water, with a hint of citrus and sugar with a bitter, coppery aftertaste that remained long after the liquid had been consumed.

"This is lemonade?" Tiger asked. "You gave us spiked lemonade?"

"This is not lemonade," I said. "The taste is off and it has a strange aftertaste. The aftertaste is—"

Char nodded.

"Blood. Specifically, my blood," she said. "As my Charkin, it's the only dragon's blood your system won't reject. I apologize for the next few moments. There is a period of adjustment that is...unpleasant."

"A period of adjust—"

A stabbing pain bloomed in my midsection as I doubled over in agony. Tiger fell to the floor next to me, groaning and grabbing her abdomen.

"Are you...are you *trying* to kill us?" Tiger managed between gasps. "This is poison."

"Don't be silly, child," Char said as she walked over. "If I wanted you dead, I could have easily managed your demise countless times in the Dungeon, or simply instructed Cynder to eject you from the top floor of her Eyrie. I wouldn't go through all the trouble of bringing you here just to poison you."

"It certainly feels like you're trying to melt us from the inside out," Tiger said through gritted teeth. "How long does...how long does this last?"

"It only feels that way...it will last much longer than you can tolerate," Char said. "Surrender to the pain. It's the only way to get through this. Dragon blood is not meant for human consumption. By all rights, it should kill you, but it won't—though you will desire death several times over before this part is done."

"Is your...your mark...it's keeping us alive?" I asked. "What is it doing to us?"

"You're expending too much energy trying to understand," Char answered. "It hasn't become painful...yet. Conserve your energy. The next phase of this gets bad."

"Gets bad?" Tiger said. "What do you mean, *gets*—?"

"Conserve?" I managed before an explosion of heat gripped my body and I groaned in excruciating pain. "This... this is—"

I never managed to finish the sentence.

The last thing I heard was Tiger's scream joining my own before the world disappeared in a gray haze of pain.

When I regained consciousness, I was laying on a small cot to one side of the floor, in the center of a large, golden runic circle. Tiger was several feet away, on her own cot inside the same circle.

"Good, you didn't die," Char said, stepping into my field of view. "We can begin."

I looked down at my body and realized I was wearing a robe similar to Char's. Tiger was dressed the same way. The mark on my hand pulsed slowly, giving off a subtle white glow in time with my heartbeat.

I felt completely refreshed with a surplus of energy and power coursing through me. I stood slowly, moving my body tentatively.

Everything felt slightly off, as if my body was too strong and too fast. It felt borrowed, as if I had stepped into a newer and stronger version of myself.

"I feel off," Tiger said. "Stronger, more powerful, but slightly off-center."

She flexed her fingers and extended her arms. Then she

squatted down and stood quickly, executing a vertical jump of nearly six feet.

She landed awkwardly and stumbled, nearly falling, but regained her balance almost instantly.

"The dragon blood did that?" I asked, feeling the power flow through my body. "Is this a permanent change?"

"What you ingested is a special drink, consider it my blood mixed with other things," Char answered. "Dragon blood, similar to human blood, it's necessary for injury recovery, infection prevention and waste removal. When placed within a human, it's usually lethal."

"And when it isn't?" Tiger asked. "What does it do?"

"It enhances everything," Char said. "Especially for someone with your healing and skin hardening abilities."

"You've made her invulnerable," I said. "Indestructible."

"Only while she's here," Char said, looking at Tiger. "This is to mitigate the damage."

"We won't be able to stop to get you medical attention," Char said, turning to me. "Some of the properties of that drink are to deal with the damage you will suffer. It has special healing properties."

"Will these properties still be present when we return?"

"No, think of this drink as an enhancer for your training," Char replied. "It allows for the trainee to exceed limits and resist catastrophic damage to the body and mind."

"You've made us stronger, more powerful, then?"

"I've changed the relativity of the scale," Char answered, confusing me. "You are both as far away from your previous self as a dragon is as far away from you in relative strength."

"So Bea could still kick my ass?" Tiger asked, disappointed. "Even with this drink in me?"

"All day every day without breaking much of a sweat," Char answered. "The difference there, is not one of power— even though she dwarfs you in power—but rather one of species. It would be like comparing a normal pitbull with a hellhound. Both are technically canines, in the strictest sense of the word, except—"

"Except one is a nearly indestructible creature of mayhem and one makes an acceptable pet," I said, thinking of Simon's bondmate. "I've seen a hellhound in action."

"Quite right," Char said. "After this transformation, you will be more than you were, the others of the Directive will sense a change in you, but will not be able to pinpoint exactly how you've changed."

"Speaking of the Directive, we can't be gone for three days," I said. "We have enemies, they will think we've been kidnapped or killed."

"Cynder will inform the rest of the Directive as to your whereabouts," Char replied. "If all goes well, you will return in three days. Just in time to meet Uluru for the exchange."

"How do you know all of this?" Tiger asked. "We just spoke to him today." She glanced at me. "It was today, right?"

"Yes," I said. "I'm curious as well. You seem well-informed about our activities as of late. How?"

She pointed to our hands.

"You are Charkin," she said. "Your location is known to me always. After that it was a matter of deduction and making a few calls."

"So we have no private life?" Tiger asked, raising a hand and showing her mark. "I mean, we can't turn these things off?"

"There is one way, well, two ways actually," Char said. "Would you like to know them?"

"No need, I'm pretty sure they involve death or removal of the limb in question," Tiger said. "Am I close?"

"Precisely correct," Char said. "Dragons do nothing by half measures—you should know this by now."

"How long will this process take?" I asked. "Seeing as how

time is not a factor in this place." I stopped to turn and examine the entire room. "How will you know when we're done?"

"I gauge time differently than you do. I will know, as will you," she said. "However, once we begin, we won't stop until we are done, or until you have both died."

"We don't get breaks?" Tiger asked.

"Bones, perhaps, but those will heal almost instantly while you are here," Char said. "I thought I was being clear? We don't stop until the process is complete or you've died. If you need rest, there is an infinite amount of time between heartbeats, if you know how to find it."

"I'm pretty sure you have to be a dragon to find that infinite amount of time," Tiger said. "I'm usually just trying to escape with my life between those two heartbeats."

"That is what you are here to change, or die trying."

Tiger remained silent while I mulled over the ramifications of this training. It was very possible Char could accidentally end us both during this process.

She wasn't exactly known for her compassion.

She was pragmatic and a realist. We needed to be trained and if we died in the process, she would shed no tears over our deaths. Nor would I expect her to. To her, it would only mean that we were not up to the demands of the training.

She was a dragon after all.

Death was a possibility I was willing to entertain, but Tiger shouldn't be subjected to this. She didn't have to do this.

"Let her go," I said, facing Char. "It's one thing to do this to me, I'm the Director of the—"

Char smiled as she turned to me.

"She is Charkin, of her own free—"Char started.

"No," Tiger said, interrupting us both. "You don't get to do this alone. If you're in, I'm in. All the way."

"Did you hear her?" I said, looking at Tiger and pointing at Char. "We don't stop until the process is complete, or until we die. There's no other option. You don't have anything to prove here."

Tiger gave me a hard stare and took a deep breath, letting it out slowly.

"I heard her, my ears are working just fine," Tiger said as she kept herself under control. "I have everything to prove."

"Not to me, you don't."

"I never said I have something to prove to *you*," Tiger said. "This is for me, not you. I have to do this for *me*. Or die trying."

I looked at Char who nodded.

"This is not your decision to make," Char said, gently placing a hand on my shoulder. "As much as it may get your knickers in a twist, you have to let her do this."

I blinked back the mild shock from Char using the 'knickers in a twist phrase' and nodded to Tiger who gave me a tight smile.

"Very well," I said. "It would seem we're ready."

"Not yet," Char said. "But you will be."

TWENTY-SIX

Char moved.

It was faster than my eyes could track and beyond what my brain could register. One moment Char was across the floor, standing in front of the large windows, with Tiger and me standing next to each other in the golden runic circle, the next, I was flying across the floor and landing in a heap on the other side of the training room.

Tiger followed a few seconds later.

"You seem to think you are here to train," Char said from across the floor, where we had been standing just a few seconds ago. "You are mistaken. You are here to fight for your lives. Demonstrate that you deserve to live. You have weapons...I suggest you use them."

Tiger jumped to her feet, unleashing a blast of kinetic energy. Char sidestepped her blasts and closed the distance, thrusting an open palm into Tiger's side and launching her sideways.

Tiger bounced across the floor with several grunts and rolled back to her feet. She had received the full impact of the attack but shrugged it off, forming her claws with a smile.

"You're still operating within what you perceive to be your human limits," Char said. "The only limits that exist in this place are self-imposed. You have access to raw power. Harness it and push past your current preconceived boundaries. Do it."

I removed my glasses and formed my twin karambits. I wasn't a brawler like Tiger, but I could hold my own in close quarters combat.

I focused my breathing and attempted something I had only tried twice in the past, unleashing the full extent of my truesight, and using it in its offensive capacity.

The few times I had attempted this at this level—using truesight as a weapon—I had failed due to my lack of power, but here, here, I could exceed whatever power I possessed. Here, I could tap into the true expression of my truesight.

Here, I could truly *see*.

Char gestured and formed a barrage of white orbs. With a nod, she sent half of them at me, and the other half at Tiger. With my truesight fully active, I was able to see Char as she was.

My mind reeled at the image. The power she harnessed was staggering, and I had no hope of processing the extent of the energy she wielded. It was beyond my imagination and comprehension.

She could, with a mere thought, vanish us from existence. We were insignificant before her, ants standing in front of a giant and just as impotent.

Two ants perhaps, but an army of ants can topple even an elephant.

She no longer appeared to be an elderly woman, but a being of light and power. My truesight didn't allow me to see into the future, but with it at its full expression, in the span of a thought I was able to see multiple potentialities, possible outcomes that formed from every one of my decisions or lack thereof.

If I stood still, a group of orbs would break my ribs and one of my legs. Raising an arm to deflect another group, resulted in compound fractures with several pieces of bone protruding through my skin.

Both those options looked painful.

With focus, I was able to *see* the path I needed to take to avoid damage. I stepped around and through the barrage of orbs as they closed on me, causing them all to narrowly miss me.

Tiger who had become far stronger according to her energy signature, batted some of the orbs away, while others hit her and bounced off her body harmlessly.

Char nodded with a tight smile as we avoided her attacks.

We continued this dance of death until I lost all sense of time. Char would attack and we would defend. The rare moments she would leave herself open, I tried to capitalize on the opportunity, only to have her change tactics and thwart my attack...painfully.

"Both of you are still reacting," she said calmly with no sign of exertion in her voice as she moved around us, deflecting our blows, sidestepping or evading our attacks. "Stop reacting. You need to fight together. Bas, you see the opening, Tiger, you exploit the opening. You must fight as one."

"There," I said, moving Tiger several feet to the side with a gentle push as Char stepped around me and right into Tiger's claws. "Strike."

Tiger drove her claws forward in a double-handed thrust.

Char didn't move and for a brief moment I feared Tiger would drive both sets of claws into Char's chest.

The next moment, Char materialized a white, wooden, rune-covered staff and slammed it into Tiger's side, with a gentle flick. I heard the ribs break and Tiger grunt in pain as the blow sent her sliding across the smooth floor.

"You should have seen that outcome," Char said, pointing at me with her staff. "You should have anticipated not just the attack, but the attack, the deflection and my response." She glanced across the floor. "Up, child. I know you were healed before you slid across the floor."

Tiger growled and closed the distance on Char.

We were going about this the wrong way.

We were two individuals fighting together against one overwhelming opponent. We needed to be two individuals fighting as one person, creating openings and exploiting the targets of opportunity.

"On me, Tiger," I yelled and she seamlessly shifted her trajectory to join me in my approach. "Two stones, one bird."

Tiger nodded and split off from me and flanked Char while I launched a frontal attack. At first, we failed gloriously and repeatedly. Char was faster, stronger, and more evasive than we ever imagined she could be, on this plane.

At some point, I couldn't say when exactly, we stopped thinking and just moved. There was no planning, no strategizing.

There were no blocks, no deflections and no attacks. Everything was one. When I moved, Tiger would react, throwing up a kinetic shield to stop a barrage of orbs, or a series of dragon punches designed to break us.

When she moved, I would redirect, seeing the path we needed to take to avoid damage from Char's counter attacks. At some point the attacks became all energy based, as Char put more distance between us and used her ability more than her staff.

Again we regressed, getting pummeled by orbs coming at us from all directions until we fell into sync again and managed to deflect and evade the orb attacks.

Once we managed that, Char transformed into a some-thing resembling a giant ogre and swatted us both across the floor with a backhand.

We were still airborne as she chased us, anticipating where we would land and drove a massive fist into the marble floor as Tiger blasted the air in front of us, and altered our trajectory slightly, causing Char to miss us by inches.

We landed in a roll and moved again. We were always moving, avoiding Char's staff, her orbs, or her transforma-tions. The most unnerving were when she transformed into one of us, throwing off our strategy by confusing me with two Tigers, or causing Tiger to deflect the wrong Sebastian as Char would transform into me, and then attack us both.

"Stop looking at the exterior and feel the energy signa-tures," Char commanded. "You cannot always believe what your eyes reveal to you."

That was when she created a duplicate of herself and they both attacked us. Without knowing which was the true Char, we resorted to attacking them both and were losing ground again.

We switched tactics and focused on one Char as Tiger covered us with a kinetic shield, preventing the duplicate Char from inflicting major damage.

With my truesight, I was able to predict the majority of the attacks and moved us out of the way enough times to prevent the duplicate from breaking through our attacks.

We continued this way for longer than I could under-stand. I felt no exhaustion, no fatigue, no hunger, my body performed flawlessly, but my mind was becoming tired.

I knew I had exceeded any perceived limits, and the few moments I was able to glance outside, everything was dark. In a moment of distraction, Char ducked under one of my slashes and slapped my chest with an open palm.

Somehow her attack had managed to get through our

defenses, through my defenses, and tossed me to one side. I landed hard on the marble floor and slid away as rage filled my mind.

Surrender and die. You know you can't win.

The voices of my past raced back at me in full force.

I screamed in outrage and jumped to my feet before closing on her, the anger filling my vision as the futility of our attacks mocked me. Char turned to face me with a small smile on her face angering me even further.

"Sebastian," I heard Tiger, her voice concerned, in the back of my mind, far away, as the mocking laughter drowned out everything else. "Not like this. You can't fight her like this."

"Step back, child," Char said, motioning to Tiger to move back. "This is where he needs to be. From this point forward this is his fight to win, or lose."

He's a Treadwell, you know they are the inferior branch of the Montagues. He can't be part of us...he's a Treadwell. He'll never amount to anything, he's a good for nothing Treadwell.

On and on the voices mocked me as I approached Char.

Char stepped back and formed her staff as I closed.

Enough of this.

I would show them. I would show this dragon, who I really was. I would show her what it meant to stand before a Treadwell.

I would show her the meaning of fear.

TWENTY-SEVEN

Heat flushed into my eyes as the full spectrum of color exploded before my vision.

My blades thrummed with power as Char deflected my attacks. I dodged her thrusts and horizontal sweeps as I moved back then feinted forward only to slide to the side.

Freak. Mutant. Outcast. You are an aberration and will never be part of this family.

The mocking laughter continued as I deflected the staff and threw one of my blades. It flew past Char's head, before I willed it back to me. I rolled forward as Char brought her staff down in a vertical strike designed to crush my head.

With my remaining blade, I intercepted the staff and angled the attack away from me. I felt one of the bones in my arm give under the tremendous force of the blow and dismissed the pain, catching the other karambit as it formed in my empty hand, shoving it up against Char's throat.

An audible gasp filled the room behind me.

"Sebastian!" Tiger yelled. "No!"

Char dropped her staff and motioned to Tiger to be silent.

"Yes," Char said. "If you strike me down, those voices will become more powerful than you can imagine. They will take you and you will be lost."

I pressed the blade against her neck harder, drawing blood.

"What do you want?" Char asked, her voice gentle. "Power, strength, dominion? Is that what you want? It's only a blade's thickness away. Take it, it's yours if you want it."

For a brief moment, it was all I could think of, all my mind screamed at me.

Cut her down and take her power! You can do it, it's yours!

I absorbed my blade as the voices became still, and I had my answer.

"Peace," I said. "I want peace."

"That...is the correct answer."

She placed a finger on my forehead, and the world exploded in a burst of white energy.

When I could see again, I lay in an extravagant but minimalist bedroom. The bed I lay in was easily an oversized Alaskan King, dwarfing everything else in the room.

The room was designed in black marble with aluminum accents and I realized we had returned to the Eyrie. The floor was black marble with flecks of silver and the intricately designed sconces were dragonheads holding crystal bulbs in their mouths, providing subtle lighting for the bedroom.

Outside I was able to view the city at night and the lights of the city that never slept were a sight to behold from this height.

"Welcome back," a familiar voice said from one of the corners. "You almost didn't make it."

Cynder.

She was sitting in a large comfortable chair, wearing a variation of the same robe Char had worn. She was facing the window and glanced in my direction as I stirred.

"Tiger," I said my voice a rasp. "What happened?"

"Tiger is finishing her training—at her request," Cynder said quickly and raised a hand, "before you think Char kept her there against her will."

"Char wouldn't do that, would she?"

"Have you met Char?" Cynder asked with a small laugh. "She would do that and more. Plus, she likes Tiger for some odd reason I just can't figure out."

"You and me both," I admitted. "I think it's because they are so much alike."

"I suggest you keep that opinion to yourself and take it to your grave," Cynder replied, looking back out into the night. "Seriously."

"Duly noted," I said, laying my head back in the comfort of the enormous bed. "Why am I here?"

"What do you recall?"

"I remember attacking Char...she was using her staff and then..." The realization rushed over me. "Oh, that's not good."

"Coming back to you, is it?"

"I had a blade against her neck," I said. "A kamikira."

"Quite deadly, even for a dragon," Cynder said. "She even allowed the scar to remain afterward. What do you think that means?"

"That my days are numbered," I said. "That's why she sent me here. It's only a matter of time before I get the best view of the city, for a few seconds, before I become bloody abstract street art below."

"That's quite graphic," Cynder said and shook her head. "You managed to cut a dragon, and not just any dragon. You managed to cut Char."

"It wasn't me."

"No?" Cynder asked the smile still on her face. "I'm pretty certain she said it was you. Are you saying she is mistaken?"

"No. I mean yes, it was me, but it was that drink she gave us," I said by way of explanation. "That dragon plasma concoction she had us drink."

"No?" Cynder asked. "That drink only allowed you to tap into the power available to you. What was done with that power...that was all you."

"I nearly killed her," I said. "What was I thinking?"

"That you had to survive," she said. "Do you recall the answer you gave her?"

"The answer I gave her?"

"When you had the blade against her neck, she asked you what you wanted," she said. "Do you recall your answer?"

"I barely recall my time there, you expect me to remember my answer to a specific question?" I asked. "Everything was a blur. I was fighting her, when she transformed into some enormous troll-like thing; then she would shift into Tiger or me, all while unleashing orbs or attacking us with that infernal staff of hers."

"Sounds like you had a grand time."

"It was not a grand time, at least, what little I can remember."

"It will come back to you," Cynder replied. "That answer under those conditions is considered a soul response. Have you ever heard of that term?"

"Never," I said. "What does that mean?"

"It's a dragon thing," she said. "The drink you were given, aside from being a disinhibitor, allowing you access to raw power and healing you from damage that would otherwise maim, or kill you, also acts as a type of truth serum—not in the context of an interrogation, but rather it causes you to face *your* truth."

"My truth?" I asked, confused. "What truth?"

"It will come back to you," she said. "That's why you're here."

"I don't understand," I said. "How long were we at Char's home?"

"Two days, give or take a few hours," she said. "Tiger should be returning soon. You still need to be reoriented, and there's the buy with Uluru. Char is cutting it kind of close."

"Reoriented?"

"Yes, you're out of sync with this plane, and your abilities are going to be off for a few hours," she said. "I suggest not using your abilities for the next few hours. We'll have Ivory come examine you and give you the all clear."

"I don't recall Ivory making house calls, ever," I said. "She's coming here?"

"She's here, just outside," Cynder said, looking at the door. "You're right, she doesn't usually make house calls, but then again, we're the House doing the calling. She makes an exception for us and we make sure her Tower remains undisturbed. It's a win-win situation for all parties involved."

"What did Char do to me?"

Cynder stood and stared hard at me.

"She made your life easier and so much harder," she said. "By making you Charkin, she increased your influence and credibility. By making you Charkin, she also made you and your second, in fact your entire Directive, targets. Her enemies will come after you to hurt her."

"Why would she increase her vulnerability that way?"

"I don't question her," Cynder said with a shrug. "She's way too old for me to tell her what to do or to question her motives. What I can say, is that she likes Tiger and she really likes you. She hasn't had Charkin in centuries. To make two? At the same time? Unheard of. Consider yourselves fortunately cursed."

"That sounds wonderfully horrible."

"Now you're beginning to understand," she said. "I'll send in Ivory and get ready for Tiger."

"Thank you," I said. "I still don't understand everything, but thank you."

"The hard part is coming," she said. "You still have to face Regina and get that gem back. I don't think either of those will be an easy task."

"On that we agree." I said with a slow nod. "You know where they both are?"

"I do and soon so will you," she said and headed for the door. "Ivory will be here shortly. Get some rest while you can."

She left the room and a few minutes later, Ivory walked into the room, with two very large assistants behind her. Behind the assistants, I saw two of her Raksashi security in full armor.

"Hello, Sebastian," Ivory said in a pleasant voice. "This should be over in a few minutes. Please remain still while I scan you and your vitals."

TWENTY-EIGHT

True to her word, Ivory was done in under ten minutes.

Whatever device or scanning equipment she used was cutting edge. She repeated most of what Cynder had said: rest for the next three hours and no using of abilities for the next six.

After that, I would be good as new.

When I asked her about the dragon plasma, she evaded giving me a direct answer which I figured was at Cynder's prompting. What she did divulge was that I would experience incremental increases in my ability in the next few months to a year.

What those increases were, she couldn't specify.

She informed me I should be aware of any changes I noticed, and contact her if anything alarming arose. When I asked her what she considered alarming, she was unsurprisingly vague.

After Ivory's checkup I drifted off to sleep again.

My dreams were filled with scenes of fighting; together with Tiger against Char, together fighting a duplicate of myself, a duplicate of Tiger, and even a duplicate of Char.

I awoke to find Tiger staring at me from the same chair Cynder had occupied earlier. In the low light, I noticed her eyes had a slight violet glow to them.

"Your eyes," I said. "Have you seen them?"

"Yours too," she said. "Have you seen them?"

"No, I haven't had the opportunity," I answered. "How are you?"

"Bruised, battered and beaten," she said with a tight smile. "Typical for spending any time with Char—this was just extra. Do you remember what happened?"

"Bits and pieces," I said. "Some parts are clearer than others. You?"

"Yes," she said. "Char didn't knock me out like she did with you. She said you were going through some kind of internal turmoil." She looked away. "You almost killed her. Do you know how bad things would have gotten if you had erased her?"

"I could imagine."

"No, you can't," Tiger said. "Cynder would have salted the earth and razed the Directive to the ground. Every single member would have been eliminated, everyone they knew and everyone those people knew, until all memory of the Directive was wiped from the earth. You've heard of six degrees of separation?"

"Yes, the idea that we are all six of fewer connections away from each other, I'm familiar."

"Cynder would've executed six degrees of extermination," Tiger said. "I'm serious. If you think Char is fearsome, Cynder is the stuff of nightmares."

"How do you know this?"

"We are Charkin," she said. "Char told me after my training. Killing the leader of a House is the ultimate betrayal, and requires the ultimate response. Everyone you know would've been targeted for execution...*everyone*."

"Bloody hell," I said, running my hand through my hair. "We were a hair's breadth from death."

"No shit," she said. "Consider that when we face Regina. I've never questioned your loyalty to the Directive, never. But this? It's not just you anymore. Every act we take impacts the entire Directive for good or bad."

"Speaking of Regina, we have a meeting with this Shadow Queen tomorrow to make the exchange," I said. "Has Cynder briefed you?"

"Not yet. She sent me in here to get sleeping beauty," she said as she got to her feet and bowed. "Is his majesty ready? I do know we leave in the morning."

"How many of the Directive can we mobilize for this?" I asked. "If we are going up against Regina and Maledicta, we are going to need—"

"No one," Tiger said, her voice serious. "This is House Char business. We are on this mission solo, just you and me."

"Stop joking," I said, with a chuckle. "Char expects us to go up against an entire darkmage assassin organization *and* Regina with no reinforcements?"

"Yes," she said completely serious. "We are Charkin. This is supposed to drive home two points—one for us and one for the world at large."

"What? That Charkin are insane and mentally unstable?"

"For us, it's supposed to make us understand what we agreed to when we accepted her mark; for the world, well, it's the same message we spread about the Stray Dogs."

"One does not cross the Stray Dogs."

"Ever. And continue to draw breath," Tiger said, getting up. "Let's go, Cynder is waiting for us. Don't forget those."

She pointed to my glasses which rested on a nightstand next to the bed. I grabbed them and put them on as we left the room.

Francis, who was waiting just outside my room, led us to a door that was on the other side of the expansive floor.

The door led to a small corridor which led to another rune-covered door, which reminded me of the runes in Char's Dungeon conference area.

"What is it with dragons and their conference areas?" Tiger asked as we walked down the corridor. "It's almost like stepping into a—"

"Battlefield," Cynder said as she opened the door for us. "Yes, we take our conference areas seriously. I'm sure Char has informed you about what has occurred in her Dungeon. The same holds true here. More blood has been spilled as a result of the conversations around this table than on the streets of this city in actual warfare."

I gazed past Cynder to the slab of wood that was the conference table. It wasn't just that the table was large, it dominated the entire room. There was enough room for the thirteen chairs that sat around it and barely little else.

Every wall was covered in runes, along with the chairs and the table itself. The table was easily ten feet in diameter and a foot thick.

Its glazed surface reflected the subtle runes from the walls and protected the surface runes from any kind of altering. I looked back and saw that the door was only about four feet wide.

I stared the question at Cynder.

"Trust me, we know some amazing teleporters," she said, closing the door behind us. "Please sit, let's make the most of the time you have."

She sat in the large black chair that was an exact duplicate of Char's white chair in the Dungeon. Being that this table was circular in design, we sat in the chairs to either side of her.

She pulled out a folder and opened it, placing the

contents on the table. I saw duplicate pictures of Regina, Uluru, and what I could only assume was Calum Kers surrounded by members of Maledicta.

I pointed to the picture.

"Calum?" I asked. "Is that him?"

"Yes," Cynder said, sliding the picture to me and doing the same with the duplicate to Tiger. "He's a formidable pyromancer who has ascended the ranks of Maledicta using the old method."

"Killing his way to the top," Tiger said. "He has the gem?"

"Had," Cynder said. "It was recently liberated by this very adept thief."

She pointed to the picture of Regina.

"Shit," Tiger said. "She's going to meet with Uluru and let him buy from her."

"Unlikely," Cynder said. "Tell her why Sebastian."

"She knows the gem is stable," I said. "Which means..."

"She's going to meet with Uluru and convince him that his best chance of staying alive is to give her the money *and* the gem," Tiger finished. "But he's a Granite Fist."

"She's had the gem for several days," Cynder said. "She hasn't assimilated it, but she has managed to enhance her ability. A darkmage Blademaster against a Granite Fist, he'd be lucky to last ten seconds."

"We're supposed to accompany Uluru on this buy," I said. "You think she's going to make a move before the buy?"

"You know her well, what do you think?"

"Once she knows where the money is, he's dead. Granite Fist or not, if she's managed to increase her power, he's gone."

"Where is Uluru now?" Tiger asked. "You have his location?"

"Yes," Cynder said. "Once he leaves this location, he's a walking dead man."

"He never left Ezra's, did he?"

"No, he didn't, and as daring as your love may be, she is not foolish enough to attempt to attack a target inside Ezra's."

"Same goes for Calum and Maledicta," Tiger added. "You can bet they're watching the place like hawks."

"Ezra's has many points of egress," Cynder said. "By the time they realize Uluru and the money are gone, it will be too late for them to act."

"Why do you leave them intact?" I asked. "Why not wipe out Maledicta like we did with Umbra?"

"Not everyone can afford the services of the Nine or my Wyverns," she said. "Before this, Maledicta served a useful purpose."

"You sent business their way as a method of control," I said. "What happened?"

"Calum happened," Cynder said. "He killed the previous leader and procured the sacred amethyst. They then felt they no longer needed our help; they would service their own clients, not live from our scraps."

"That's called a bad business decision," Tiger said. "When did it get bad?"

"It was a situation I was willing to tolerate in the short term, until Calum incinerated one of our security operations to prove how vulnerable we were and how superior they were."

"You can't let this go," I said. "It's a loss of face."

"Worse, he attacked an operation directly connected to me and I am directly connected to Char," she said. "Any weakness shown taints the House and no one crosses House Char and gets to continue breathing."

"Why not take them down yourself?" I said. "You're certainly powerful enough."

"What do you think I'm doing?" Cynder said with a malicious smile. "I'm sending two Charkin to resolve this issue with the utmost prejudice. I will give you everyone's location. You bring me the sacred amethyst and Calum. I don't care what you do with your love—consider that my gift to you."

"That's gracious of you," I said. "What would be the standard OP?"

"The standard operating procedure for an insult of this magnitude would be to unleash the nocturnal eclipse."

"That's real?" Tiger asked. "I thought that was a myth."

"Char said no?"

"It was Char's first suggestion," Cynder said. "Do you know what that would mean?"

"Everyone involved dies, no mercy, no compassion," I said. "No one who is part of this sees the sun ever again. Hence the eclipse."

"I explained that your Regina would be part of that group, and Char capitulated," Cynder said with a small shake of her head. "I'm sorry. I didn't think she would go this far. I thought that by informing her of Regina's involvement, she would merely spare her, but she opted on a different course of action altogether."

"She decided to send her two new Charkin to resolve the situation, make a statement and leave it up to me if Regina lives or dies," I said. "Is that about right?"

"Yes," Cynder said, her voice hard. "This is not Directive business. You are acting as Char's weapons and only answer to her in this. The Councils, the NYTF, any and all authorities are superseded by Char in this operation. Do you understand?"

"Do they understand this?"

"It will suffice that you two do," she said. "They will be informed on a need to know basis."

"And right now they don't know, wonderful," Tiger said. "Slash me sideways, why not turn on the blender and ask us to stick our hands in? It would be less painful."

"The message must be sent and dragons have not and do not ask for permission," Cynder said, her voice still hard. "We act and then we deal with the repercussions if anyone is still left alive to deal with."

"We're not going to go on a wholesale killing spree," I said. "Even if it is for Char."

"You know the terms—she expects the sacred amethyst and Calum delivered to her or me," Cynder clarified. "Regina's fate is left in your hands."

"And the Granite Fist?" Tiger asked. "He was an arrogant ass, but he was mostly okay."

"Try to keep Uluru alive, I don't need additional grief with the Granite Fist," Cynder said. "However, I know these situations suffer collateral damage. Whether he lives or dies depends entirely on you two."

She pulled out another folder from under the table and placed it on the surface.

"Everything you need is in here," she said, tapping the surface of the folder. "Your vehicle has been fully equipped with weapons and any amenities you might require. Do I need to go over the consequences of failure?"

"You do not," I said, placing my hand on the folder. "We know how these operations function."

"Let me guess," Tiger asked, risking our lives. "Not an option?"

"Not even remotely," Cynder said. "You may go."

TWENTY-NINE

"We don't give Regina the chance to intercept Uluru before the buy," I said as Tiger drove downtown to Ezra's. "That's one opportunity lost which means—"

"She'll be forced to act during the buy itself, especially if she sees us there," Tiger finished. "Do you think we would be enough of a deterrent? Maybe she will take the money and just leave the city?"

"Don't forget Maledicta," I said. "Calum will want the amethyst back and he won't be afraid to kill for it."

"Great, and Uluru has to buy this gem for his leader who probably doesn't care who dies in the process as long as he gets his amethyst."

"Power does strange things to people," I said, looking over the logistics of the operation. "The power of an Archmage is quite the incentive."

"Sure, you only have to be willing to sacrifice your life to get it," Tiger said. "They don't even know how stable it is. It could be stable for a day or a year, and then BOOM—no more mage."

"They're not thinking about that part," I said. "It's the

allure of the power. That is what's driving them. What they could do with that power. Who they could control or eliminate. It doesn't matter that they have crossed Char, they either don't know, or they know and don't care. With the power of an Archmage, facing a dragon would be feasible."

"Not Char," Tiger said, keeping her voice low. "You felt her power. Do you think an Archmage would have a chance against her?"

"Yes, for all of three seconds," I said. "Even Cynder would be a threat to an Archmage. Dragons are not to be trifled with."

Tiger nodded as she swerved around traffic.

"Give me the run down," she said as she sped downtown. "We get Uluru first then?"

"We head to Ezra's first, tonight," I said. "Uluru is supposed to meet with this Shadow Queen at first light to make the buy."

"Why not do it at night?" Tiger asked. "It's what I would do."

"That's why," I said. "Whoever it is, this Shadow Queen is trying to act against expectations."

"*Whoever* it is?" Tiger asked. "C'mon, we both know it's Regina."

"When I see her face or sense her energy signature, then I will confirm the identity," I said. "Until then, this Shadow Queen is an unknown variable, one we have to account for."

"I'll account for her by driving my claws into her leg."

"Really?"

"I could have said chest or neck," Tiger said. "Impaling her leg is me being nice."

"Let's refrain from any impaling until we know who it is we are impaling," I said. "It's safer that way."

"I don't really do safe."

"I know."

We arrived at Ezra's a few minutes later.

Tiger parked the Tank out front.

"If anyone was waiting for us, they know we're here now," I said, looking around the front of the property as we disembarked.

"The Stray Dogs don't hide," Tiger said as the Tank locked with a clang and an orange wave of energy crossing the surface of its chassis. "Besides, we don't have Regina, Uluru, or the money, why would they attack us?"

I turned as the front door of Ezra's opened.

Uluru stepped out of Ezra's and approached us holding a medium-sized Zero Haliburton silver case handcuffed to one hand.

"We now have Uluru and what I'm assuming is the money," I said, turning at the growl from across the street. "And company."

"Company?" Tiger said as she turned. "Shit, that's a whole lot of ugly heading this way. Get in the car. Now!"

I helped Uluru into the car and locked it. No one except me or Tiger could unlock the Tank once it was locked.

Uluru was saying something, but I couldn't hear his words. Once locked, the Tank was completely soundproof.

From across the street, I saw a massive ogre close on us. It towered over Tiger as she crossed the street to intercept it.

While that was happening, I unleashed my innersight and scanned the area. Darkmages were out in force on the roofs of several buildings and in the side streets around us. Maledicta was wasting no time. Somehow they knew that Uluru or the money he carried, led them to the amethyst.

Why would Ezra let Uluru out into the street, where he would be vulnerable and defenseless, especially with this welcoming committee?

He didn't let him out where he would be vulnerable and defenseless. He let him out into our care. He knew we would protect him.

Several darkmages approached from the sides, shaking me out of my thoughts.

"You don't want to do this," I said. "Go home or go back to your headquarters. You don't want any part of this."

"Tough talk from one mage," one of the darkmages said. "We are Legion. Even if you defeat one of us, we will swarm you and snuff out your life."

"I count five of you," I said, moving back so that my rear was covered by the wall behind me. "Do you know who I am?"

"We don't and we don't care," the same darkmage spoke again. "Give us the Fist and we may leave you alive. On second thought, give us the Fist and we'll end you quick."

"I recognize that car," another of the darkmages said. "This is one of those Directive mages—What's the name again? Treadstone, Treadbell, Tread something, bunch of academics who think they're heromages of some kind."

"Treadwell," I corrected, "and tonight, you are mistaken."

"Oh, the mage is upset we got his name wrong," the first darkmage mocked. "I'll make sure to carve it on your face when I kill you."

All five drew short swords.

Each of the blades were rune-covered and glowed a faint orange in the night.

I formed my karambits and let a small growl escape my lips. They paused in their approach.

"Tonight, I don't represent the Directive, tonight I'm on official duty."

"For who? The Library?" first darkmage answered. They all laughed in response. "Kill this idiot."

They began closing on me.

"No, tonight I'm doing official business for House Char."

"What the hell?" another darkmage said. "Did he just say—?"

He never finished his sentence as I sliced through his leg. He collapsed, ending his attack in the midst of groans and cries. My attack galvanized the rest and they mobilized.

My innersight wasn't nearly as potent as my truesight, but it allowed me a degree of foresight, as I evaded the blades and sliced through legs and arms.

The attack lasted all of ten seconds.

I managed to leave them all alive, and if they managed to get medical attention, they would survive the night. If not, they would bleed out in front of Ezra's inside five minutes.

My mercy extended only so far to enemies who were doing their best to cut me down to size. I glanced at the now shocked Uluru and signaled to him to stay put as I ran into the street to join Tiger.

The ogre roared and smashed a fist into the ground where Tiger had stood a moment earlier.

I stepped in and sliced its arm and it roared in pain, swinging an arm in my direction. I ducked and rolled to the side, avoiding the attack and giving Tiger a moment to breathe.

We both backed up and put some space between us and the ogre.

"Maledicta must be well connected to have access to ogres," I said, circling the creature. "They must have some mages in their ranks."

"Where do you get an ogre anyway?" Tiger asked. "It's not like there's some ogremart in the city somewhere. Are they grown?"

"They are created, and you don't want to know how, really," I said. "We need to go. Can you stop this one, or do I need to go get an Eradicator from the Tank?"

"Oh, now you want to use an Eradicator?" she asked, giving me a dirty look and rolling her shoulders as she approached the ogre. "When I wanted to use one, you were all rules and regulations. One ogre, and you want to blow up half the street."

"It's an ogre," I said, backing up to the Tank. "You got this?"

"I said—" she ran forward and unleashed a kinetic blast as she drove a fist into the ogre's chest, and through it. The ogre looked down at Tiger, raised a fist overhead to drive it into her head and froze in place, collapsing backward into the street, leaving a stunned Tiger looking from the ogre to her fist in shock. "I got this?"

"I said stop it," I called out from the Tank, as I opened the door. "Not make it Swiss cheese. We need to go before more of these darkmages arrive. Now!"

She ran over to the Tank as I started the engine.

We strapped in and I pulled away from Ezra's. I really hoped Ursula wouldn't be too upset at the mess we had just created.

"One punch!" Uluru said from the back. "Yes! That was a strike worthy of the Granite Fist. You were not this powerful when we fought. I know this in my bones. How did you get so strong in three days? You must show me your training methods."

"They're a little unorthodox," Tiger said, removing a wipe from the glove compartment and removing the blood and gore from her arm. "That was...unexpected."

"Quite the understatement," I said. "It would seem Char's method of training has had some lasting side effects. Uluru."

"Yes?" he said. "How can I assist?"

"Is that the money handcuffed to your wrist?"

"Yes," he said warily. "I cannot give it to you."

"I don't want you to," I assured him. "The negation sphere is inside as well?"

"Yes," he said with a quick nod. "Both are secure inside. I am to meet the Shadow Queen at first light."

"Change of plans," I said. "Someone knew you were at Ezra's and let Maledicta know. If any of those who just attacked me survived—"

"Why did you not kill them? They are enemies."

"I do not kill indiscriminately," I said an edge to my voice. "Not for you, not for anyone."

"I understand," he said with a nod. "This is your code."

"Yes," I said. "Thank you. Can you contact this Shadow Queen? We have to change the meet."

"She will not like this," he said then paused as if giving it thought before nodding to himself, "but we have been compromised. We must make a change. One moment."

He pulled out a phone and pushed one button. I assumed it was a burner phone precisely for this buy. It probably only had one number programmed into it.

"Hello," a computer-manipulated voice answered. "We are not to meet until first light. Why are you calling me?"

"The Cursed Ones attacked me," Uluru said. "We must change the meeting."

Silence.

After a few seconds, the voice answered.

"Very well, do you remember the alternate location?" the voice asked. "Do not say it out loud."

"Yes, I remember it," Uluru said. "Do you want me to go there?"

"No, I want you to send your bodyguards there," the voice said. "They will make the buy for you. Maledicta has you tagged somehow. They're still clean. Can you hear me, driver?"

"Yes," I said. "What are your instructions?"

"Drop off the Granite Fist at the next corner," the voice said. "After he unlocks it, take the case from him."

"My sect will not approve of this," Uluru said. "They will not give the money to—"

"You trusted these two with your life," the voice said. "Are you saying your life is not worth twenty million and a negation sphere?"

"That and more," Uluru said. "What do you want?"

"For you to follow instructions."

"Very well, what am I to do?"

"Good, give the driver your phone and unlock the case. Get out at the next light," the voice said. "I will give the driver the amethyst and he will give me the money and the sphere. Your sect will get what it wants, and I will get what I want. We all win tonight."

"I do not like this," Uluru said, but unlocked the cuff affixing the case to his wrist. He unlocked the case and showed us the money before handing the case to Tiger. "I will trust you."

"Smart man," the voice said, but Uluru was looking at me. "Do what is right or my life is forfeit."

I pulled the Tank over at the next light and unlocked it. Uluru stepped out. I glanced in the rear-view mirror. He remained focused on us as we drove away. He was placing his life in my hands, and the weight of that decision rested heavily on my shoulders.

"Where to?" I said as we pulled away. "He's gone."

"I know. It's only you two?" the voice asked. "Where's your backup?"

"It's only us two."

"That was foolish," the voice said. "Doesn't matter, this ends tonight."

"Where do you want to do this?" Tiger said. "We have your money, do you have the amethyst?"

"I do," the voice said. "Roosevelt Island, lowest level of the Motorgate Garage, right off the Roosevelt Island Bridge. You have one hour or I'm gone and the amethyst is gone with me."

"We can't get to Roosevelt Island from here," I said. "We're going to have to drive into Queens and double back onto Roosevelt Island. That's easily a ninety minute drive."

"Then I suggest you drive faster," the voice said. "Fifty-nine minutes."

The call ended.

THIRTY

"This is a deliberate ploy," Tiger said checking the map on her phone. "Whoever it is, this Shadow Queen thinks we have backup. We can't mobilize them and make it there in one hour."

"I think that's the plan," I said. "Strap in, we're going to have to bend some laws to make this meet on time."

"Whatever you do, do not attract the NYTF," she said. "We don't need that kind of grief tonight."

I sped up 1st Avenue, running several red lights and risking an NYTF pursuit. Several red light cameras flashed behind us as I didn't bother to stop at the intersections.

It didn't matter.

The Tank didn't have plates that could be traced to anyone. I accelerated and motioned to Tiger to look up. If our caller was able to track our progress as they alluded to earlier, then they had some kind of surveillance.

I was figuring some type of drone with hi-tech camera equipment, probably infrared or something equally advanced. Tiger pulled out some sophisticated binoculars provided by

SuNaTran, and peered up through the moonroof. After a few minutes she gave me a thumbs up.

"A drone of some kind," she said, still looking up through binoculars. "Cutting edge with some major camera equipment. That's all I can tell."

"Good enough," I said, turning onto the Queensboro Bridge and heading into Queens. "How much time?"

"Thirty-five minutes," she said, her voice tight. "You need to go faster."

"Bloody hell," I said, tightening my straps. "Hold on."

"Shit, you're going to press the button?"

"No choice. As soon as I hit a straight away, we fly."

"If you get this wrong, we die."

"With twenty million," I said. "What a way to go."

"Not funny," she said, holding onto the hand rests. "Do not smash us to little bits."

I turned off the bridge exit and made a right onto 21st Street. I flicked up the red cover on the dash and glanced at Tiger who nodded and cursed under her breath.

Making sure there was no immediate traffic in front of us, I flipped the switch. The hydraulics in the Tank lowered the chassis to a few inches above the street and the turbocharger kicked in, unleashing a piercing whine, while the engine itself roared, shooting the Tank forward as the speedometer raced upward.

We managed eighty miles an hour under a second and I was questioning Cecil's sanity when we crested past one hundred.

"This is too fast!" Tiger yelled. "We're going to overshoot the turnoff to Roosevelt Island!"

I had engaged the brakes half a minute earlier and we were slowing down. It was just taking too long.

"You need to give us a cushion. 36th Street is five blocks away! We're not going to stop in time," I yelled back as I fought to keep control of the steering wheel. "Throw up a kinetic—"

"I know what I need to do," she yelled in response. "Keep us straight. If you deviate from the street, the shield will flip us. Understand?"

I nodded and focused on the driving.

She leaned out of the window and for a brief second I thought the velocity would rip her out of the Tank and into the street. She hooked her legs around the seat and cast a large kinetic shield.

The Tank started to slow.

Several blocks later, we slowed down to the reasonable speed of sixty miles an hour, made our turn on 36th Street and crossed the Roosevelt Island Bridge with fifteen minutes to spare on the allotted time limit.

"You know this is a trap," she said as we entered the Motorgate Garage. "There's no way this Shadow Queen is here alone."

"I know," I said, driving down to the lowest level. "We'll play it as it comes. I don't enjoy being toyed with."

"You know the saying," Tiger replied as she pulled out the Eradicator. "One does not—"

"Cross the Stray Dogs," I finished as we arrived on the lowest level. I turned off the engine and looked ahead at the lone figure standing at the other end of the garage, looking at her watch.

"Showtime," Tiger said. "Let's do this."

THIRTY-ONE

We stepped out of the Tank and stood in front of it.

The figure across from us gave us a small golf clap. She stood in between several columns and kept her gaze fixed on us.

"That was impressive," she said. Her voice was still modulated behind a dark mask she wore, but from her figure, I could tell she was female. "You made it on time."

I held up the case.

"Your money," I said. "The amethyst?"

She held up a small black pouch that radiated power. Even from this distance, there was no question it was the real thing.

"How do you want to do this?" Tiger asked, her voice tense. She was on high alert and with good reason. The entire garage was filled with energy signatures. "Hand us the amethyst."

"Give them the money first and I'll hand you the amethyst," she said and pointed behind us. "Consider it an act of good faith. If you move slow, they promise not to slice and dice you."

"What did you say?" I called out. "What was that?"

"Give them the money and you won't be hurt," she said, angry now. "Do it, now!"

I glanced at Tiger who gave me a knowing glance back and nodded. Darkmages from Maledicta surrounded us with blades drawn. I handed one of them the case.

"Good. Now bring me the money," she said, pointing to one of the darkmages. "Tonight, would be good."

One of the darkmages ran over to where the Shadow Queen stood and handed her the case. She briefly opened it and closed it again after making sure the money was there.

From behind one of the columns stepped out Calum.

"I hate to deal and run, but my part in this is done," she said and tossed the black pouch holding the gem to Calum with a bow. "As promised, enjoy your newfound power, Archmage Calum."

"Thank you," he said with a smile. "Finally."

She ran behind the columns and disappeared from sight as Calum laughed and pulled out the amethyst. He grabbed it in one hand and let his flames engulf the gem.

"He's absorbing the amethyst," Tiger said as she focused her breath. "We can't let him finish the process."

"That's not the threat," I said under my breath. "You go after Regina, feel for an abnormal energy signature, similar to that gem, but stronger. Go, now."

"Are you sure?"

"As if our lives depended on it," I replied with a growl. "Don't let her escape."

Tiger exploded from the mob of darkmages with a blast of kinetic energy and took off after the Shadow Queen with the swarm of darkmages behind her, giving chase.

What they intended to do when they caught up to her still remained to be seen. I removed my glasses and looked down the garage.

"You don't want to do that," I said. "That is a bad idea."

"That is the voice of cowardice," Calum said. "Who sent you after me? The dragons? They will learn to fear me after tonight and you have helped me achieve my goal. After tonight, I will be stronger than Cynder, stronger than Char even."

"I hate to break this to you, but you've been tricked," I said. "That's not the real sacred amethyst."

"Liar," he said and formed several orbs of flame around his body. "Even now my power is enhanced. I will reach Archmage soon and all will kneel before me, starting with you."

He unleashed several orbs in my direction.

I twisted my body using my truesight and evaded the orbs as they crashed into his darkmages, destroying them instantly. Screams filled the garage and the stench of burning flesh assaulted my senses.

"Stop this!" I yelled. "You're killing your own men!"

"They mean nothing to me," he yelled back, creating more orbs. "They are expendable, I have all the power I need. Here"—he raised his hands—"in my hands, is all I need."

More orbs flew out from his hands, forcing me to take cover behind the concrete columns. Some of the darkmages weren't so lucky as orbs crashed into them, incinerating them where they stood.

This was no normal flame. It appeared to be some combination of runic flame with a variation of napalm that adhered to its targets and burned even through the metal of the cars in the garage.

The screams were excruciating as the darkmages fell. Calum laughed as more of his men died. I had to stop him. I fully unleashed my truesight and hoped I had even a fraction of the ability I possessed at Char's home.

I stepped out from behind the column and dodged an orb which slammed into a darkmage behind me, ending him. I ran and slid behind another column that was closer to Calum and made my way to where he stood.

Several columns and a few near misses later I was one column away.

"Come you, dragon pet," Calum mocked. "I want them to find your charred body when they come looking for you. See what I did there? Your charred body?"

"Very clever," I called out and received a barrage of orbs against the column I used as cover for a response. "If only you were slightly more clever to know the gem you absorbed was a fake."

"Lies!" More orbs crashed into the column and I could feel the blast of heat on the other side. "I felt the energy signature. My power is increasing. Feel for yourself, Charkin pet."

I let my senses expand and he was right, his energy signature was increasing. For a moment, a sliver of doubt crept into my mind and then I saw it. There was an aberration in the energy around his body.

It was subtle and I doubted anyone who didn't possess my ability would catch it. It was a masterful counterfeit but the gem he absorbed was flawed, much like the man himself.

"Why would I lie?" I called out. "I don't stand to gain anything from lying to you."

"Of course you do," he sneered. "You want to recapture your woman, your Shadow Queen. Did you know it was Regina Clark? Oops, she didn't want you to know, apologies."

Shit. After her slice and dice comment, I had been fairly certain it was Regina. Now I was certain. I really hoped Tiger didn't kill her.

"If you let me help you, we can get that thing out of you before it's too late."

"Get it out of me?" he yelled as more orbs of flame crashed into the column. "Are you listening to yourself. You want me to voluntarily relinquish this power? The power of an Archmage?"

By this point, any Maledicta who hadn't been incinerated, had fled the garage.

"You still have time, Calum," I said. "Listen to me. It's not too late."

"It is too late...for you," he said, forming what I imagined was the largest flame orb he had ever created. Even from where I hid, I could feel the heat reaching me. "It's time for you to die, Charkin. Time for a new leadership to rule this city. Time for me to ascend and for the dragons to die."

It was now or never.

I ran out from behind the column and let my truesight guide me. Calum had released some smaller orbs before releasing the enormous orb he held before him. I dodged the small orbs and closed the distance when Tiger appeared behind him.

He was so focused on me that he didn't sense her until it was too late. I saw she carried a limp Shadow Queen in one arm as she unleashed a fist at Calum's head. It connected with a solid thump and he crumpled to the ground unconscious, or at least, I hoped he was unconscious.

This was the same Tiger that had recently punched a hole through an ogre. She could have easily liquefied Calum's brain with that strike.

As he collapsed, I noticed that his monster orb of flame had not dissipated. In fact, it hovered in the air for a few seconds and then began heading my way.

I looked around, but found no exit.

The nearest exit was several ramps up from our location. When that orb exploded, we would be standing inside a concrete oven. Everything on this level would be disintegrated.

I looked at Tiger who scooped up Calum and ran to my location, dumping both Regina and Calum on the ground.

"Huddle close," she said. "You better hope the lessons I learned at Char's stuck. If not, we are so dead."

The orb picked up speed as Tiger stood in front of me and gestured, forming a super dense dome of kinetic energy. It was so dense I could see the air wavering around us as she poured energy into it.

The orb raced along the ground, giving off so much heat that the concrete floor cracked in its wake as it headed straight for us.

"I really hope you learned those lessons," I said as the orb drew closer. "If we don't make it out of this, it's been an honor."

"Right back at you," she said and hugged me as the orb crashed into her dome.

The world exploded in a roar of flame and heat. The dome held until the walls caved in, smothering the orb and trapping us underground.

THIRTY-TWO

"Over here," someone yelled. I vaguely recognized the voice and saw a familiar face look down into the debris of what was left of the lower level of the garage. "They're alive!"

The face of a relieved Uluru was looking down at me.

"Does he have to yell?" Tiger said, holding the side of her head. "We can hear you. Stop yelling."

"Step aside," another voice said, and there was no mistaking the tone. It was Beatrix. "Where is he?"

She looked down into the hole and saw an unconscious Calum lying on the ground next to me.

"Alexander," I heard her say. "Make room."

"One sec," I heard Alexander's deep voice respond. "Step back. All of you down there, cover your heads."

We did as instructed and a large crash filled what was left of the garage. The concrete and debris were immediately removed, and we stood in the center of an open clearing. All of the cars in the garage had been converted to slag, all except the Tank, which was covered in dust and debris, but remained intact.

Cecil was truly a master of his craft.

"Alexander, remove the pretender and retrieve the amethyst," Beatrix said. "Cynder is expecting us within the hour."

Alexander bent down and scooped up Calum effortlessly.

"One moment," I said. "I have a blood debt with the Wordweavers to get that amethyst back. I have no desire to feel the consequences of a broken blood debt."

Beatrix turned, gave me a look and let a hand hover over Regina.

"Does she live or die?" Beatrix asked me. "Your choice."

"Can't you remove the gem without killing her?"

"No," Beatrix said, shaking her head. "She has assimilated the gem. If I remove it, she dies. I can, however, leave it within her and neutralize its properties. You can then hand her over to the Wordweavers, fulfilling your blood debt. Make your choice."

"And Char?" I asked. "How will she—?"

"If the command is given to end her life, would you stand by and accept the verdict quietly?" Beatrix asked. "Or would you fight?"

"I would fight."

"Even if it is Char who commands it?"

"Even if it is Char," I said. "Even if it costs me my life."

"Exactly so," Beatrix replied with nod. "This is why you are Charkin. A dragon does not ask for permission. A dragon acts and deals with the consequences, whatever they may be."

"Neutralize it," I said, looking at Tiger who nodded. "I'll deal with the consequences."

"We will," Tiger said. "Whatever they may be."

"So you shall," Beatrix said as a blast of violet energy slammed into Regina, suspending her in the air, as the energy engulfed her entire body. After a few moments, Regina fell gently to the ground. "It is done."

Alexander clapped me on the shoulder and grinned at me.

"Well done," he said. "It was an even split on you surviving this mission. I was rooting for you."

"Who was rooting against?" I asked.

Alexander pointed to Beatrix with his head.

"I am pleased you survived, but I am a realist," she said. "Your odds of survival and a successful completion of all objectives were slim to none. I am glad you managed slim. You both show promise."

"Thank you, I guess," I said, leaning against the Tank. "What are you going to do with him?"

I pointed to Calum.

"You don't want to know," Alexander said. "Cynder wants to have some words. Most in his position don't survive conversations with Cynder."

"We will speak again soon...Charkin," Beatrix said after a pause and held out her hand. Inside it, resting on her palm were two small pins of a dragon in mid-flight. "Wear them proudly. You earned them."

"Thank you," I said, giving one of the pins to Tiger who bowed. "I didn't expect—"

"It was my honor," she said, bending down to lift Regina up. "She will need to be under observation to make sure the neutralization took effect. Char will want to see her as well. When she is ready for guests, you will be summoned."

"Thank you again," I said with a bow. "I do appreciate it."

"Don't thank me yet," Beatrix said with a small smile. "You will still have to explain yourself to Char about your choice."

"I'm not looking forward to that."

"You're finally learning," Beatrix said. "We will see you soon. Until then, do try to avoid any mischief."

She gestured and all four of them disappeared in a green flash.

I looked around and found what I was looking for—the

silver case. I grabbed it and handed it to Uluru who smiled and clasped my hand before giving me a hug.

"The Granite Fist is your brother for life," he said and handed the case to some of the other Granite Fists behind him. "We must leave now."

"You didn't get the gem, I'm sorry."

"Do not be," he said. "Power easily attained is easily lost. I am now the new leader of the Granite Fist in my region. Our previous leader has fallen to greed and corruption. My sect brothers and sisters have cast him out."

"Sounds like the right decision," I said, heading to the passenger side of the Tank. "I wish you a safe journey home."

"And you as well, my brother," he said. "If you need the Granite Fist, all you need to do is call, and we will be there."

He put his two fists together and bowed deep. The rest of the Fists behind him did the same. Tiger got into the Tank next to me.

"Breakfast at Ezras's?" she asked, starting the engine with a throaty roar. "It's just about time."

"Absolutely not," I snapped, then took a deep breath. "Sorry, that's how this whole mess started. Breakfast at Ezra's. Let's have breakfast at the Church. Even if I have to make it myself. It's safer this way."

"Those sound like famous last words," she said and weaved her way out of the wreckage of the garage. "Once I get home, all I need is a hot shower and a long nap, maybe two or three days' worth."

I laughed as we arrived on the surface and headed home.

THE END

AUTHOR NOTES

Thank you for reading this story and jumping into the world of the Treadwell Supernatural Directive with me.

Disclaimer: The Author Notes are written at the very end of the writing process. This section is not seen by the ART or my amazing Jeditor—Audrey. Any typos or errors following this disclaimer are mine and mine alone.

Like an onion.

Both Sebastian and Tiger are layered. Tiger's layers seem to be violence with a side of pain and a dash of agony. Sebastian is holding in a metric ton of rage and disguises the anger behind the facade of responsibility.

Out of the two, Sebastian is the more dangerous. He reminds me of that person where everything seems fine until that one fateful day when it's not, and Armageddon has been scheduled.

Like one of the bystanders in Ezra's said: He woke up and chose today to be his last day. That pretty sums up Sebastian.

Whereas Tiger is just an unleashed force of nature that will undo everything she encounters.

What a pair.

It was an absolute blast to write this story and I do hoped you enjoyed it as well.

I really enjoyed the notes and answers to the questions on this story. They ranged from it started too abruptly, to, some parts felt like filler, and then to everything flowed the way it needed to. It was excellent!

To give you my thoughts on these (and other thoughts about the story structure), I'll share my two cents.

Yes, it probably started too abruptly (reminds me of T&B as we started running down a street chasing a werewolf with no explanation whatsoever lol!) and the some of the cast weren't explained as thoroughly as expected (the first crew that blows up and Maledicta). Usually when that happens in my stories, those of you that have been reading the stories for a while know it means there's more to come in later books.

There's more to come in later books.

Maledicta is not gone, neither is Regina. Things are going to get complicated and deadly as they should. As for the filler parts, I can totally understand the sentiment. Not that I agree with it, I've never written filler parts in a story (at least not consciously). If something feels like filler then it means you may have missed a deeper meaning, or its going to be explained later. I ask that you be patient and please hang on for the ride. I almost wrote please hang on for dear life.

The next book, ENDGAME TANGO will be coming soon.

Too many things need to be resolved and the Stray Dogs are going to face an enemy that knows how they operate and who they are...all of them. Their very existence is being threatened and they must stop this enemy or the Directive is done.

Things will get darker, questions will be answered, more questions will be raised and some characters may not make it to the end of the story...we will see.

I had plenty of fun with Char and Cynder in this story. No, they are not the same person and each serves a distinct purpose—again, layers are in play. Why would the information broker handle key aspects of training and not the enforcer? Why would the enforcer neutralize a gem she was instructed to retrieve?

Hmmm...questions, questions.

By now you know the answer...layers.

In ENDGAME TANGO those questions will be addressed. It won't be easy, it won't be pleasant, and it won't be expected. It won't be a smooth ride for the Stray Dogs, but it will definitely be an exciting one.

If there was one word to describe ENGAME TANGO it would be...betrayal. Hold on and strap in. It's going to be a bloody, bumpy ride, and the Stray Dogs will never be the same again.

Ok deep breath....whew.

I wanted to take a moment to thank you in exploring the Stray Dog's world with me. This is something of a departure from M&S and as I like to say, this world is a bit more brutal and deadly. You've allowed me the space to roam the streets with Sebastian and Tiger(and survive it) and for that I am humbly grateful.

Anytime I write something other than M&S, I run the risk of writing something incredibly polarizing. The amazing and great thing is that I have the most spectacular readers on the planet who not only allow me the space to do this, but actively encourage me and nudge in those directions with ample support.

You all totally rock!

If you gotten this far—thank you. I appreciate you as a

reader and a daring adventurer, jumping into these imaginings of my mind, and joining me as we step into these incredible stories and worlds.

You are amazing!

Thank you again for jumping into this story with me!

BITTEN PEACHES PUBLISHING

Thanks for Reading!

If you enjoyed this book, would you please **leave a review** at the site you purchased it from? It doesn't have to be long… just a line or two would be fantastic and it would really help me out.

Bitten Peaches Publishing offers more books and audiobooks

across various genres including: urban fantasy, science fiction, adventure, & mystery!

www.BittenPeachesPublishing.com

More books by Orlando A. Sanchez

Montague & Strong Detective Agency Novels

Tombyards & Butterflies•Full Moon Howl•Blood is Thicker•Silver Clouds Dirty Sky•Homecoming•Dragons & Demigods•Bullets & Blades•Hell Hath No Fury•Reaping Wind•The Golem•Dark Glass•Walking the

Razor•Requiem•Divine Intervention•Storm
Blood•Revenant•Blood Lessons•Broken Magic•Lost
Runes•Archmage•Entropy•Corpse Road

Montague & Strong Detective Agency Stories
No God is Safe•The Date•The War Mage•A Proper
Hellhound•The Perfect Cup•Saving Mr. K

Night Warden Novels
Wander•ShadowStrut•Nocturne Melody

Rule of the Council
Blood Ascension•Blood Betrayal•Blood Rule

The Warriors of the Way
The Karashihan•The Spiritual Warriors•The Ascendants•The
Fallen Warrior•The Warrior Ascendant•The Master Warrior

John Kane
The Deepest Cut•Blur

Sepia Blue
The Last Dance•Rise of the Night•Sisters•Night-
mare•Nameless•Demon

Chronicles of the Modern Mystics
The Dark Flame•A Dream of Ashes

The Treadwell Supernatural Directive
The Stray Dogs•Shadow Queen

Brew & Chew Adventures
Hellhound Blues

Stay up to date with new releases!
Shop www.orlandoasanchez.com for more books and
audiobooks!

CONTACT ME

To send me a message, email me at:
orlando@orlandoasanchez.com

Join our newsletter:
www.orlandoasanchez.com

Stay up to date with new releases and audiobooks!
Shop: www.orlandoasanchez.com

For more information on the M&S World...come join the
MoB Family on Facebook!
You can find us at:
Montague & Strong Case Files

Visit our online M&S World Swag Store located at:
Emandes

For exclusive stories...join our Patreon!
Patreon

Please follow our amazing instagram page at:
bittenpeaches

Follow us on Youtube:
Bitten Peaches Publishing Storyteller

If you enjoyed the book, **please leave a review**. Reviews help the book, and also help other readers find good stories to read.

THANK YOU!

ART SHREDDERS

I want to take a moment to extend a special thanks to the ART SHREDDERS.

No book is the work of one person. I am fortunate enough to have an amazing team of advance readers and shredders.

Thank you for giving of your time and keen eyes to provide notes, insights, answers to the questions, and corrections (dealing wonderfully with my extreme dreaded comma allergy). You help make every book and story go from good to great. Each and every one of you helped make this book fantastic, and I couldn't do this without each of you.

THANK YOU

ART SHREDDERS

Amber, Anne Morando, Audrey Cienki, Avon Perry
    Bethany Showell
    Chris Christman II

Denise King, Diane Craig, Dolly Sanchez, Donna Young Hatridge

Hal Bass

James Wheat, Jen Cooper, JillyJack Ripley, Joy Kiili, Julie Peckett

Karen Hollyhead

Larry Diaz Tushman, Laura Tallman I

Malcolm Robertson, Maryelaine Eckerle-Foster, Melissa Miller, Michelle Blue

Paige Guido

RC Battels, Rene Corrie, Rohan Gandhy

Sara Mason Branson, Sondra Massey, Stacey Stein

Tami Cowles, Tanya Anderson, Ted Camer, Terri Adkisson

Vikki Brannagan

PATREON SUPPORTERS

TO ALL OUR PATRONS

I want to extend a special note of gratitude to all of our
Patrons in
The Magick Squad.

Your generous support helps me to continue on this amazing
adventure called 'being an author'.
I deeply and truly appreciate each of you for your selfless act
of patronage.

You are all amazing beyond belief.
***
If you are not a patron, and would like to enjoy the exclusive
stories available only to our members...join the Squad!

The Magick Squad

THANK YOU

Alisha Harper, Amber Dawn Sessler, Angela Tapping, Anne Morando, Anthony Hudson, Ashley Britt

Brenda French

Carl Skoll, Carrie O'Leary, Cat Inglis, Chad Bowden, Chris Christman II, Cindy Deporter, Connie Cleary

David Smith, Dan Fong, Davis Johnson, Diane Garcia, Diane Jackson, Diane Kassmann, Dorothy Phillips

Elizabeth Barbs, Enid Rodriguez, Eric Maldonato, Eve Bartlet, Ewan Mollison

Federica De Dominicis, Fluff Chick Productions, Francis August Valanzola

Gail Ketcham Hermann, Gary McVicar, Geoff Siegel, Grace Gemeinhardt, Groove72

Heidi Wolfe

Ingrid Schijven

Jacob Anderson, James Wheat, Jannine Zerres, Jasmine Breeden, Jeffrey Juchau, Jim Maguire, Jo Dungey, Joe Durham, John Fauver, Joy Kiili, Joy T, Just Jeanette

Kathy Ringo, Kimberly Curington, Krista Fox

Leona Jackson, Lisa Simpson, Lizzette Piltch

Malcolm Robertson, Mark Morgan, Mary Barzee, Mary Beth Wright, Marydot Pinto, Maureen McCallan, Mel Brown, Melissa Miller, Meri, Duncanson

Paige Guido, Patricia Pearson, Patrick Gregg

Ralph Kroll, Renee Penn, Robert Walters

Sammy Dawkins, Sara M Branson, Sara N Morgan, Sarah Sofianos, Sassy Bear, Shelby, Sonyia Roy, Stacey Stein, Steven Huber, Susan Spry

Tami Cowles, Terri Adkisson, Tommy

Van Nebedum

Wanda Corder-Jones, Wendy Schindler

ACKNOWLEDGEMENTS

With each book, I realize that every time I learn something about this craft, it highlights so many things I still have to learn. Each book, each creative expression, has a large group of people behind it.

This book is no different.

Even though you see one name on the cover, it is with the knowledge that I am standing on the shoulders of the literary giants that informed my youth, and am supported by my generous readers who give of their time to jump into the adventures of my overactive imagination.

I would like to take a moment to express my most sincere thanks:

To Dolly: My wife and greatest support. You make all this possible each and every day. You keep me grounded when I get lost in the forest of ideas. Thank you for asking the right questions when needed, and listening intently when I go off on tangents. Thank you for who you are and the space you create—I love you.

To my Tribe: You are the reason I have stories to tell. You cannot possibly fathom how much and how deeply I love you all.

To Lee: Because you were the first audience I ever had. I love you, sis.

To the Logsdon Family: The words *thank you* are insufficient to describe the gratitude in my heart for each of you. JL, your support always demands I bring my best, my A-game, and produce the best story I can. Both you and Lorelei (my Uber Jeditor) and now, Audrey, are the reason I am where I am today. My thank you for the notes, challenges, corrections, advice, and laughter. Your patience is truly infinite. *Arigatogozaimasu.*

To The Montague & Strong Case Files Group—AKA The MoB (Mages of Badassery): When I wrote T&B there were fifty-five members in The MoB. As of this release, there are over one thousand five hundred members in the MoB. I am honored to be able to call you my MoB Family. Thank you for being part of this group and M&S.

You make this possible. **THANK YOU.**

To the ever-vigilant PACK: You help make the MoB...the MoB. Keeping it a safe place for us to share and just...be. Thank you for your selfless vigilance. You truly are the Sentries of Sanity.

Chris Christman II: A real-life technomancer who makes the **MoB Kaffeeklatsch** on YouTube amazing. Thank you for your tireless work and wisdom. Everything is connected... you totally rock!

To the WTA—The Incorrigibles: JL, Ben Z., Eric QK., S.S., and Noah.

They sound like a bunch of badass misfits, because they are. My exposure to the deranged and deviant brain trust you all represent helped me be the author I am today. I have officially gone to the *dark side* thanks to all of you. I humbly give you my thanks, and...it's all your fault.

To my fellow Indie Authors: I want to thank each of you for creating a space where authors can feel listened to, and encouraged to continue on this path. A rising tide lifts all the ships indeed.

To The English Advisory: Aaron, Penny, Carrie, Davina, and all of the UK MoB. For all things English...thank you.

To DEATH WISH COFFEE: This book (and every book I write) has been fueled by generous amounts of the only coffee on the planet (and in space) strong enough to power my very twisted imagination. Is there any other coffee that can compare? I think not. DEATH WISH—thank you!

To Deranged Doctor Design: Kim, Darja, Tanja, Jovana, and Milo (Designer Extraordinaire).

If you've seen the covers of my books and been amazed, you can thank the very talented and gifted creative team at DDD. They take the rough ideas I give them, and produce incredible covers that continue to surprise and amaze me. Each time, I find myself striving to write a story worthy of the covers they produce. DDD, you embody professionalism and creativity. Thank you for the great service and spectacular covers. **YOU GUYS RULE!**

To you, the reader: I was always taught to save the best for last. I write these stories for **you**. Thank you for jumping down the rabbit holes of *what if?* with me. You are the reason I write the stories I do.

You keep reading...I'll keep writing.

Thank you for your support and encouragement.

SPECIAL MENTIONS

To Dolly: my rock, anchor, and inspiration. Thank you...always.

Larry & Tammy—The WOUF: Because even when you aren't there...you're there.

Stacey Stein: For: Don't ask me why they hate me... Great quote, thank you.

Orlando A. Sanchez

www.orlandoasanchez.com

Orlando has been writing ever since his teens when he was immersed in creating scenarios for playing Dungeons and Dragons with his friends every weekend.

The worlds of his books are urban settings with a twist of the paranormal lurking just behind the scenes and with generous doses of magic, martial arts, and mayhem.

He currently resides in Queens, NY with his wife and children.